THREE

(plus one)

TALES OF DIZ AND CLARISSA

Ann McMan

Bywater
BOOKS

Ann Arbor
2016

Bywater Books
PO Box 3671
Ann Arbor, MI 48106-3671

www.bywaterbooks.com

For Lucy, who taught me the virtue of patience.
I miss you every day.

THREE

(plus one)

TALES OF DIZ AND CLARISSA

THREE

(plus one)

Nevermore!

"1-800-SPANK ME. I know that number." Diz was staring at the caller I.D. readout on her cell phone.

Clarissa glanced at her. "You should. You practically have it on speed dial."

Diz snapped her phone shut and tossed a malted milk ball at Clarissa. Christmas was only a few days away, and the office break room was inundated with tins full of cheap confections from vendors.

It was a good throw. It landed in Clarissa's coffee, causing it to slosh all over the article she was proofreading.

"Oh, *nice* one, nimrod." Clarissa snatched up the top pages and shook them off over her waste can. "Great." She held up the top page. Spidery blue lines from what had been notes were running down the sheet of paper like varicose veins. "You can be such an *asshole*. Now I'll have to do this all over again."

Diz shrugged. "You impugn my integrity and then take umbrage when I defend myself?"

Clarissa sighed. "Eighteen people in this department, and I get to share a rabbit hutch with *you*. Someday I'm going to figure out who I pissed off in a previous life."

Diz snapped her bright red suspenders and stuck out her tongue.

"Oh, *that's* mature. And what's with the outfit today? You look like Howdy Doody on crack."

Diz rolled her eyes. "Give me a break, Clar. It's for the Christmas party. Besides, you wouldn't know Howdy Doody if he walked up and bit you on your high-class ass."

Clarissa opened her mouth to reply just as her phone rang. She turned away from Diz and snapped it up. "Research, this is Clarissa Wylie."

Diz watched her while she talked. She and Clarissa had been working together for nearly two years, now. They weren't exactly friends—not in the sense that they ever did much together socially.

But that wasn't hard to understand. Clarissa came from money—old money. And her family owned the company that published the magazine they worked for. In fact, her family's company published half the goddamn magazines printed in the U.S.

Clarissa was a comer. Everybody knew that. Since finishing grad school at Princeton, she was paying her dues by working her way up through the ranks of the family business. One year in subscription services, eighteen months in distribution, and a whopping two years in research with Diz. Her next move would certainly be to a private office upstairs in the editorial suite. But you had to give her credit— she worked hard, and she knew her shit.

Diz, on the other hand, was pretty much fated to remain chained to her desk in the bowels of the building, vetting facts and making sure the Wylies didn't get sued for libel or plagiarism. That was okay. This was just her day job. At night, she slaved away on her other passion—a comprehensive and comparative study of the development of detective fiction as a literary genre. She was A.B.D.—all-but-dissertation—and after six years of night school, she was only nine hundred plus pages away from earning her doctorate in American literature from the University of Baltimore.

Dr. Gillespie—what a nice ring that had. Of course, she'd always be Diz to her family and friends. The childhood nickname started out as an homage to her father's love of jazz, but it stuck. And frankly, it suited her a whole lot better than her given name.

And once she finally had that sheepskin? Well. She'd blow this pop stand and . . . and what?

And be an unemployed Ph.D.

Oh, well. There were worse things. She could end up like her idol. Poe died alone in poverty at age forty, about five blocks away from this goddamn building.

She glanced at Clarissa, who was still talking. Correction, listening. She was jotting notes down in longhand, using that damn, precious Italian fountain pen of hers.

Diz studied her. It wasn't the first time.

Clarissa wasn't just a comer, she was a looker, too. Her thick auburn hair cascaded down her back like a red waterfall. And she had a set of legs that would make Betty Grable's pale by comparison. She knew how to dress for them, too. Today she was wearing a form-fitting black suit and stylish shoes that probably cost more than Diz spent on clothing in a year. Correction—in *five* years. Although she admired the view, Diz wondered why Clarissa bothered. It wasn't like anyone who mattered was going to see her down here in this dank basement.

Clarissa turned her head and caught Diz staring. She frowned and tossed a paper clip at her. Diz caught it. Diz always caught anything Clarissa tossed at her, except compliments, of course. Diz usually let those fly by like fastballs that were thrown outside the strike zone. It was better for Diz not to indulge in how great it felt when Clarissa paid attention to her. That was one dead-end street that she just didn't need to travel. Everyone knew that Clarissa was A.B.E.—all-but-engaged. And her intended was the granite-jawed, heir-apparent to Baltimore's oldest and most prestigious shipbuilding company. It was going to be one hell of a merger, and photos of the glamorous couple frequently punctuated the society pages of the *Sun*.

No, Diz thought, as she gazed back at Clarissa's smoky gray eyes. *There was no there, there for her.*

Clarissa hung up her phone.

"What time are you leaving for the party?" she asked.

Diz shrugged. "Sometime after six. I figure it'll take forty-five minutes to get there with all the Christmas shoppers clogging the Metro."

This year's party was at Nevermore!—a high-end tapas bar at the Inner Harbor.

"You're taking the Metro? Why don't you take a cab?"

"A cab?" Diz raised an eyebrow. "Sure . . . I mean, I don't really have to *eat* the rest of the month."

Clarissa sighed. "Ride with me. I've got a car."

"Of *course* you do."

"Don't be a cretin. You'd be doing me a favor."

Diz was intrigued. "How so?"

Clarissa looked like she was trying to decide whether or not she wanted to answer that question.

"Oh, dear," Diz guessed. "Trouble in paradise? You and Dash Riprock have a falling out?"

"Go fuck yourself."

Diz sighed. "I usually do on Friday nights."

Clarissa shook her red head. "Why do I bother with you?"

Diz gave her a blinding smile. "Because I'm a foot taller than you, and whenever we go anyplace together, people think you're out with Rachel Maddow."

Clarissa thought about that. "Sad, but true."

"So." Diz adjusted the black horn-rims that used to make her look like a nerd, but now made her look chic. "What's up with Dash? He not coming to the party?"

Clarissa shrugged. "He has to work late."

"On the Friday night before Christmas? What? Is there a late-breaking shipment of yard arms coming in from Norway, or something?"

"Or something." Clarissa smiled. She had a great smile, with big, deep dimples that made Diz go weak at the knees if she looked at them for too long. It was every bit as hypnotic as staring at a lighted candle, and every bit as dangerous, too. If you weren't careful, you'd end up going blind.

Diz sat back in her chair and extended her long legs. She was wearing her best pair of red, high-top Chucks. They matched her suspenders perfectly. "Let me get this straight. You need *me* to keep you company until Lord Nelson arrives?"

"Something like that," Clarissa said.

"What makes you think I don't already *have* a date? Or two?"

Clarissa rolled her eyes. "If you do, I promise not to cramp your style. Besides, aren't you likelier to make friends with someone at the party? If memory serves, you fared quite well last year. What were their names, again?"

"I have *no* idea who you're talking about."

"Oh, yes, you do. I'm talking about those two *zaftig* types from the mail room."

Enlightenment dawned. "Oh. You mean Randi and Ronni. The *twins*. How could I forget?"

14

"Beats me," Clarissa offered. "As I recall, you walked with a limp for most of a week."

"And I thought you didn't care."

"In your dreams."

Clarissa had no idea how true that statement was.

"Well," Diz said. "It's true that I do like to keep my options open. So you're in luck. I don't, as it happens, have a date for tonight. Yet."

Clarissa smiled at her. "Great. Then maybe you'll consent to keep me company until Dane arrives?"

Diz narrowed her eyes. "I'm curious about something, Clar."

"What's that?"

"Why hang out with me? Why not just mosey on up to the head table, where the rest of the 'fambly' will be tossing back the single malts?"

"I don't socialize with my father at work."

"This isn't work. This is a Christmas party."

"Maybe for you. For me, it's work."

"Well that kind of sucks."

Clarissa shrugged. "I'm used to it."

Diz smiled at her sadly. "I know. That's the part that sucks."

Clarissa stared at her for a moment. She opened her mouth to say something when Marty Jacobs appeared in the doorway to their cube.

"Yo—Diz. A couple of us are gonna splurge and share a cab ride to the Harbor. Wanna come along?" He glanced at Clarissa, then lowered his voice. "Lisa even volunteered to sit on your lap if you promise *not* to behave."

Diz glanced at Clarissa, who seemed to be studying something fascinating on the sleeve of her jacket.

"No thanks, Marty. I've made other plans."

"Dude." Marty looked incredulous. "I don't think you heard me. I said *Lisa*, as in the woman voted *Miss Sweater Meat of 2011*."

"I *heard* you, Marty," Diz hissed. "Tell Lisa I'm beyond flattered, but I've made other plans."

Marty stood there looking back and forth between Diz and Clarissa. Then he shook his head. "Whatever floats your boat. Don't say I didn't ask."

"I won't."

"Later." He rapped the wall of their cube and backed out, headed for god knows where.

Diz looked at Clarissa who sat there regarding her with a raised eyebrow.

"Miss Sweater Meat?" she asked.

Diz shrugged.

Clarissa shook her head. "I guess it's an acquired taste."

Diz fought to keep her gaze away from the plunging neckline of Clarissa's silk blouse. Telling Clarissa that she could certainly hold her own in a Sweater Meat contest would probably be a bad idea.

A *very* bad idea.

"Yeah," she said instead. "I guess."

❊ ❊ ❊

The party at Nevermore! was in full swing.

Or was that full swig?

Most of the management echelon decamped as soon as the dancing started.

Diz didn't really blame them. The majority of the dancers were beyond rhythmically challenged, and their obscene gyrations made them look like drunken extras from the set of *Mogambo*.

Across the table from her, Clarissa just looked amused. She was sipping on a glass of Pinot Noir, or Petit Syrah, or *something* red and expensive, and Diz was amazed at how long she could make one glass of anything last.

Diz was feeling *no* pain, and not just because of the five vodka gimlets she'd had. Dash/Dane was still a no-show, and Clarissa didn't really seem to mind, nor did she appear to be in any particular hurry to leave.

Diz could feel a surge of false courage pushing against the levy of better sense that normally kept her out of harm's way. And that couldn't be good news.

After three drinks, Clarissa started to look less formidable. After *five*, she started looking downright . . . attainable. And Diz was barely

16

clinging to enough good sense to realize that it was in everyone's best interest for her to change the circumstances—fast.

Idly, she wondered where Lisa was. Maybe it wasn't too late to rethink that whole lap-dance idea.

The music was so damn loud that it was hard to think. And she needed to be able to think. She needed to think because right now, all she wanted to do was *act*.

She heard Clarissa say something, but the ambient noise was too loud for her to make out what it was. She leaned toward her.

"What?" she bellowed.

Clarissa met her halfway. Bad idea. This was far too close for comfort. Her eyes were like tractor beams.

"I said, do you want to dance?" she repeated.

Diz looked around at the crush of people standing near their small table. No one seemed to be looking her way.

"With whom?" she asked.

Clarissa rolled her eyes. "With *me*, nimrod."

Diz wasn't sure she heard her correctly. "Did you say with *you?*"

"Is there an echo in here? Yes. Dance. You. With me."

Diz stared at Clarissa with her mouth hanging open.

"Oh, for god's sake," Clarissa finally said. She grabbed Diz by the hand and yanked her to her feet. "Come on. It won't kill you."

Diz could feel the room starting to spin.

"I'm not so sure this is a good idea," she said, as Clarissa pulled her toward the dance floor.

"I think you can handle it," she said, tightening her hold on Diz— probably so she couldn't fall. Or flee, which was likelier.

Diz wasn't feeling particularly strong right then, and she appeared to be leaking courage like a giant sieve.

Clarissa led them to a spot on the dance floor that was mostly unoccupied. Someone slammed into Diz from behind and shoved her up against Clarissa. She ended up with a mouthful of red hair, and Clarissa grabbed on to her suspenders with some kind of death grip. The sensation of having all that silk-clad sweater meat plastered up against her was making her woozy. She had a feeling that this wasn't going to end well.

17

The music changed. Lady Gaga now.

Great.

Red Wine. I've had a little bit too much.

Clarissa laughed. "This should be my theme song."

Diz could feel the vibration of her words against her ear. She drew back and looked at her. They weren't so much dancing as swaying. There wasn't really much room to move around.

"Seriously? You've had, like *one* glass, all night."

Clarissa rolled her eyes. "It's a metaphor, asshole."

Diz was confused. "For what?"

Clarissa just shook her head and tugged her closer. "You're a bright girl. Figure it out."

Diz was going to reply, but she got distracted when she noticed that people were staring at them. *Lots of people.* It started out small, then seemed to spread out across the dance floor like a wave. Between gyrations, they were pointing and talking behind their hands.

She bent closer to Clarissa's ear. "People are staring at us."

"You only just noticed that?" Clarissa replied.

Diz nodded. Clarissa's hair smelled great—like red violets.

"Why are they looking at us? Is my fly unzipped or something?"

Clarissa laughed. "Is your fly on your *ass?*"

Diz had to think about that. In fact, her fly was quite happily conjoined with the waistband of Clarissa's tight skirt. Right now, it was one hundred and eighty degrees away from her ass.

"No."

"Then I don't think it's related to your pants."

"Well what the hell is it then?"

Clarissa pulled back and gave Diz an ironic look. She raised a hand and ran it through Diz's thick head of short, dark hair.

"They think you're Rachel Maddow, nimrod."

"Oh." Diz had a sudden, and brief, moment of clarity. "*That.*"

"Yeah. *That.*"

"Lucky you."

Clarissa smiled and tugged her forward. "No argument from me on that one."

Someone slammed into them again.

This time, the perpetrator stopped and apologized.

"Hey, sorry about that," he said.

Diz lowered her chin and looked at him over the rim of her glasses. He appeared to be anything but sorry.

"No problem," she said.

The guy continued to stand there, staring at them. "You're Rachel Maddow, aren't you? Man . . . I *knew* it was you. You totally don't look this tall on TV."

Clarissa started to laugh.

Diz rolled her eyes. "Well. You know how those cameras distort everything."

"This is so freaking cool," the guy said. "I don't really watch the news much, but I've seen you on Leno."

"Right," Diz said. "I'm really proudest of my late night TV work."

"Hey. I won't bug you anymore."

"Thanks," Diz said. She turned away from him and started to steer Clarissa off the dance floor.

"What's the matter, *Rach?*" Clarissa asked. "Don't you like dancing with me?"

"You call that dancing?" Diz asked. "It was more like roller derby. Why don't we just find a doorway to stand up in, or a deserted closet? At least we'd end up with fewer bruises."

"Well, that depends on what you have in mind," Clarissa said.

Diz stopped and stared at her. "Do I know you?"

"Not as well as you could." Clarissa gave her a look that could only be described as sultry. And Diz was sure about that because she checked.

Twice.

Tunnel vision. Isn't that what it's called when everything around you suddenly constricts into a tiny pinhole through which you can see only *one* thing?

That's how Diz felt. And she wasn't sure if it was because of the booze, or due to the insane realization that she was moving in to kiss Clarissa—who halfway seemed to be inviting it.

"There you are," a voice behind them roared. "I've been looking all over this place for you."

Dash Riprock. Of course. He'd have to show up at precisely *this* moment.

Diz dropped her chin to her chest.

Clarissa didn't look exactly ecstatic to see him, either.

Dane Nelson looked like he'd just popped out of a ten-best list in *G.Q.* He looped an arm around Clarissa's shoulders and kissed her on the hair.

"Hi ya, babe. Sorry I'm late."

Diz noticed that he was holding a half-empty martini glass. Apparently he wasn't *that* desperate to find her.

Clarissa glanced at Diz, then looked back at Dane. "I gave up on you."

From your mouth to god's ear, honey.

Dane laughed, revealing a set of perfect teeth. They looked blue in the neon light.

"Hey, I got here as soon as I could." He looked around the crowded place. "Where's your stuff? I'm beat. Can we get out of here?"

"You remember Diz, don't you?" Clarissa asked.

Dane glanced at her. Diz could see his eyes moving up and down her frame.

"Sure. Hi, Diz. Thanks for keeping my girl company."

"No problem, Dash."

He didn't appear to notice the nickname, but Diz saw the corners of Clarissa's mouth twitch.

"Look," Diz said. "I'm kind of beat myself, Clar. I think I'll call it a night."

Clarissa looked disappointed. "You're leaving?"

Diz nodded. "You don't need a chaperone anymore, and I definitely don't need anything else to drink. I'll see you on Monday, okay?"

She started to turn away but Clarissa laid a hand on her arm.

"At least let us give you a ride home?" She looked at Dane, who took the hint.

"Oh. Sure. Yeah. We'd be happy to drop you off." He drained his glass and set it down on a nearby table.

Asshole.

"No thanks," Diz said. She looked around until she saw Marty holding up the bar. "I'll just share a cab home with Marty."

"And Lisa?" Clarissa asked.

Diz looked at her in surprise. Clarissa dropped her gaze.

"Maybe," she replied. "If I'm lucky." She held up a hand and gave them a brief salute.

She walked away, cursing herself for her stupidity. What the hell had she been thinking? Clarissa was just using her to kill time until Lord *fucking* Nelson showed up. And she had almost blown it. If Dane hadn't appeared precisely when he did, Diz would've ruined everything. Clarissa certainly would have slapped her, and tomorrow's headlines in the *Huffington Post* would've been all about how Rachel Maddow got dumped in a Baltimore nightclub.

Marty saw her and waved her over.

"Diz." He looked behind her. "Where's the Duchess?"

Diz jerked her head toward the door. "Prince Charming finally showed up."

"Sweet." He looked her over. "So you're finally on work release?" He signaled the bartender. "Let's have another round. What are you drinking? Gimlets?"

"Nothing else for me, dude. I'm already half toasted."

"Fuck that shit. It's Friday night, and the company is picking up the tab."

The bartender appeared.

"I'll have another T&T." Marty gestured at Diz. "And she'll have a Goose Gimlet." He looked at Diz and frowned at her morose expression. "Make hers a double."

"Jesus, Marty. You'll have to pour my ass into a cab."

"Yeah. So? What are friends for?" He raised his glass. "We'll have just *one* more drink, then we'll head out."

Right. Whatever.

Three drinks later, Diz was past the point of no return. She knew she was in trouble when a server reached over her to retrieve a platter of hot—something—from the bartender. The steam from the dish wafted up into her face, and she felt the room start to spin.

Marty saw it.

"Oh, Christ, you're gonna hurl, aren't you?"

He quickly picked up his glass and pushed away from the bar.

Diz clapped a hand to her mouth and nodded. She slipped off her stool and staggered toward the restrooms, gaining speed as she pushed her way through the crowd, which parted like the Red Sea before the staff of Moses.

Apparently, she wasn't the first person to make this trip.

In the solitude of a bathroom stall, she let go of everything, including what was left of her hope and dignity. Then she sagged to the floor and cursed her miserable life.

This is what it always came down to, she thought. *This is what you got if you let yourself believe in fairy tales.*

A pair of heels appeared outside the stall. Someone tapped on her door.

Great.

"Just a second," Diz muttered. "I'll be right out."

She managed to haul herself to her feet and took a quick look to be sure there was no mess to clean up.

Diz always cleaned up her messes.

With shaking hands, she opened the door.

Clarissa was standing there.

Diz was stunned. *Was this some kind of fresh delusion?*

"You look like shit," Clarissa said, without a trace of empathy.

Nope.

She was real all right. And she was mad as hell. Her face looked like a thundercloud.

"What are you doing here?" Diz pushed past her and headed for the sink.

"I came back to get you. I had a feeling you'd do this."

"Do what?" Diz bent over the sink and rinsed out her mouth with cold water.

Clarissa walked up behind her. "*This.* Act like a stupid frat boy." She grabbed a stack of paper towels and reached around her to wet them. Then she wrung them out and pressed them to the back of Diz's neck. It felt great.

"Yeah, well . . . apropos of frat boys, where's Dash?"

Clarissa shrugged. "I dropped him off at home."

"Your home?"

"*His* home—not that it's any of your business."

Diz stood up and turned around to face her. Clarissa kept the damp towels against the back of her neck. That meant she continued to stand awfully close. As nice as that was, Diz felt like it was risky. Her stomach was still doing somersaults. The bright light in the bathroom was making her head swim. The scent of red violets wasn't helping much, either.

"I think I need to go lie down," she said.

Clarissa actually smiled. "You think?" She laid a hand on Diz's forearm. "Can you walk?"

Diz nodded.

"Let's go. My car is right out front."

Diz didn't have the stamina to argue with her. "Okay."

Five minutes later, Diz was snugly strapped into the soft leather passenger seat of Clarissa's Alfa Romeo.

They were driving along West Pratt Street, away from the harbor. Clarissa took a right on South Paca and drove past the main campus of the University of Baltimore.

"My home away from home," Diz muttered.

"What did you say," Clarissa asked.

Diz shook her head. "Nothing." She ran her hand along the wood grain dash of the car. "What is it with you and all the Italian stuff?"

Clarissa shrugged. "I like simplicity. I like beautiful things." She smiled. "I like things that are simply beautiful."

Diz snorted. "No kidding."

Clarissa looked at her. "No kidding."

Shit. There was that stomach thing again.

"I think you need to stop," she rasped.

Clarissa checked her rearview mirror, then roared over to the side of the road. "If you puke in this car, I'll kick your ass," she cautioned.

Diz was fumbling with her seatbelt.

"Jesus." Clarissa reached over and unhooked it. Red violets. It was too much. Diz fell out of the car and staggered to her feet. She made it as far as somebody's parked Mercedes, slid down the hood, and tossed her cookies all over its front tire.

She felt a set of cool hands on her forehead. They held on to her until she finished.

"Come on," Clarissa said. "We're almost there."

She helped Diz stand up and guided her back to the car.

"Where are you taking me?" Clarissa didn't live in this part of town. She lived in a high-rise condo, near Boston Street Pier.

"I'm taking you home."

"You know where I live?"

Clarissa looked at her. "Of course."

Diz wanted to ask how, but it was too complicated. She was amazed at her ability to be coherent at all.

"I don't suppose you have a bottle of Lavoris stashed somewhere in this thing, do you?" she asked.

Clarissa actually smiled. "No. But I think there might be some Tic Tacs in the glove box."

Diz opened it and fumbled around inside the uncommonly large compartment. *Italians must have to carry a lot of shit around,* she thought. She pulled out a rolled up pair of torn pantyhose.

She held them up. There was a gaping hole in the thigh area of the left leg.

"Care to explain these?" she asked.

Clarissa glanced at them. "No. I really don't."

"Hmmm. Okaaayyy."

"It's not what you think," Clarissa said.

"Since you don't *know* what I think, you don't really get to say that."

"I can imagine."

"I bet you can't."

Clarissa sighed. "Okay. What do you think?"

Diz rolled them back up. "I can only imagine *two* explanations. One—Dash was in an *incredible* hurry, and these got snagged on one of his diamond-studded cufflinks."

"You have a rich fantasy life, don't you?"

"I'm starting to develop one."

Clarissa shook her head. "What's your other explanation?"

"Ah. You wear these on your head while you indulge in your secret passion for knocking over mini-marts. Evidence suggests you're very good at it."

Clarissa thought about that for a moment. "I *do* love Twinkies."

Diz looked at her smugly. "Inspector Dupin's got nothin' on me."

She put the pantyhose back into the glove box and continued to rummage around until she found her prey.

"Voila." She pulled out a white plastic box and shook it. Then she held it up to read its label. "Oh, great. *Citrus.* Just what I need."

"Beggars can't be choosers, Diz."

Diz shook out a handful of the tiny mints and popped them into her mouth.

"Ugh. Maybe I should just chew the pantyhose?"

"I always knew you were a pervert."

Ten minutes later, they were parked in front of Diz's brick row house. Her condition had deteriorated dramatically. Clarissa got out and walked around to open her door.

"Keys?" she asked.

"Pocket," Diz said. She didn't carry a purse.

"You expect *me* to look for them?" Clarissa asked.

Diz nodded.

Clarissa sighed. "Stand up, then." She helped Diz climb out of the car.

Diz leaned against Clarissa as she fumbled around in her front pockets.

"This is kinda nice," Diz muttered against her hair.

"Don't get any ideas, nimrod."

"I won't," Diz promised. "Not any new ones, at least."

Clarissa held up the keys. She took hold of Diz's arm. "Can you make it up the steps?"

"I think so." Diz took a shaky step forward, then stopped.

"Oh, god, you're not going to be sick again, are you?" Clarissa asked with alarm.

"No. Just want to savor this. Can we go slow?"

Clarissa sighed. "Sure."

They slowly climbed the steps. Diz leaned heavily against Clarissa while she fumbled with the keys.

"If you don't have a car, why do you have so goddamn many keys?"

"You know, for someone with such a classy background, you sure do curse like a sailor."

"Yeah?" Diz groused. "It must be from spending two years in a basement with *you*."

Clarissa finally found the right key and unlocked the door. They stumbled inside. Clarissa stopped dead in her tracks while she looked around the spacious interior. It was tastefully appointed with primitive antiques and colorful artwork.

"Whatssamatter?" Diz asked.

"This place is *gorgeous*."

"You sound surprised."

Clarissa looked at her. In the soft lamplight, her eyes looked more hypnotic than usual, and that was saying a lot. Diz got an idea. Well, it was a repeat of the same idea she'd had earlier at the club. She leaned toward her, but gravity wasn't cooperating. She missed her target and kept going. Clarissa barely caught her.

"Come on, Casanova. Where's your bedroom?"

"That was fast," Diz slurred. "I was at least gonna make us drinks."

Damn, she smelled good. Diz dropped a sloppy kiss on her neck. "I really like you," she muttered.

Clarissa steered them toward the stairs. "I really like you, too. And I'll like you a whole lot more when I can get your clothes off. You smell like a brewery."

Diz continued to nuzzle her neck as they made halting progress up the stairs. "You wanna get me naked? I've *always* wanted to get you naked."

"Really? I hadn't noticed." Clarissa pushed Diz's hand away from her breast. "Step. Step. One more. That's right. You can do it."

You bet I can do it, Diz thought.

They were nearly at the top landing. Diz was feasting on her neck now. And she'd managed to work her free hand back inside Clarissa's jacket. It was soft and warm in there. Everything about Clarissa felt soft and warm.

Next thing she knew, she was falling backwards, and Clarissa was right on top of her. They landed on the bed with a soft thud.

Clarissa pushed up on her forearms.

"Good god, you're a pain in the ass." She sat all the way up and straddled Diz. "And a heavy one, at that." She unhooked her suspenders and started to unbutton her white shirt. "Let's get these dirty clothes off you."

"I'm dirty?" Diz was busy groping any part of Clarissa she could reach.

Clarissa batted her hands away in between manipulating buttons and zippers. "Yes, you're dirty. And I must be crazy."

"Why are you crazy?" Diz asked with a yawn.

"Because," Clarissa pulled off Diz's shirt and backed away to tug down her trousers, "against all reason, I seem to like it."

Clarissa stood up next to the bed and removed Diz's shoes. Then she pulled her pants the rest of the way off. Diz was now clad only in her bra and panties. Clarissa hastily pulled a blanket up to cover her.

"You need to go to sleep now," she said. She removed Diz's glasses and put them on the nightstand.

"I don't wanna sleep." Diz reached for her. "I wanna snuggle."

"You want to *snuggle?*"

Diz nodded sleepily. "Please?"

Clarissa glanced at her watch.

"*Please?*" Diz made her biggest, puppy-dog eyes. "I promise you I'll behave."

Clarissa rolled her eyes. "Sure you do."

"I *promise,* Clar." Diz yawned again.

Clarissa deliberated for a minute. Then she sighed and knelt on the edge of the bed. "Okay, but only for a minute. I *mean* it."

Diz smiled through her haze of inebriation and happy delusion. She held up the blanket in invitation.

"I must be in my dotage," Clarissa said as she kicked off her shoes and lay back against her.

Diz wrapped her up in her arms. God she felt great. They fit together perfectly.

"Clar?" she asked, stifling another yawn.

Clarissa turned her head on the pillow to look at her. Their noses were practically touching.

"What?" Her voice was soft and low.

"Thanks."

Then Clarissa kissed her. Or she kissed Clarissa. She wasn't sure which one of them started it, but it didn't really matter. The kiss went on and on, until Diz felt herself floating away. She was aware that her head had dropped onto Clarissa's shoulder, then she wasn't aware of anything but the faint, sweet scent of red violets.

❀ ❀ ❀

When the morning came, Diz was sure of three things. One, she was alone in her bed. Two, something clearly had died in her mouth. And three, she would never drink *eight* vodka gimlets again. Ever.

She lay on her back and stared up at the ceiling of her bedroom. She had a vague recollection of Clarissa bringing her home, and an even vaguer recollection that she'd done some drunken groping on the stairs. She closed her eyes in mortification.

The longer she lay there, the more she remembered. One nightmare succeeded another until they were too numerous to count.

Oh, Jesus Christ. She undressed me.

Diz lifted the blanket and gazed down at her scantily clad form. *Thank god.* At least she still had her underwear on.

But there was something else. Clarissa had been on the bed with her. She was sure of it. *And they kissed.* She raised a shaky hand to her lips. She was sure of that, too.

Wasn't she?

Shit, who even knew? The whole thing could just be some kind of drunken wish fulfillment. It wouldn't be the first time for that. She was so damn pathetic.

She gingerly rolled over to test her equilibrium. Not too bad, considering.

She caught a trace of something on the pillow. Red violets. *Holy shit.* It was then that she saw the shoes . . . Jimmy Choo's . . . on the floor next to the nightstand. Clarissa's shoes.

Oh my god. She was *here. She's* still *here.*

Either that, or she left without her fucking shoes . . .

28

"You're awake."

Diz looked up at the doorway. Clarissa stood there, holding a tall glass of something. She walked to the bed.

"Can you sit up? How's your head?"

"Which one?" Diz pushed herself up into a sitting position and tugged the blanket up to cover her chest.

"Here." Clarissa held out the glass. "Drink this."

Diz eyed her with suspicion. "What is it?"

"Don't ask. It's a home remedy. My father swears by it."

Diz recalled being amazed by the number of single malt Scotches Bernard Wiley blew through during the ninety minutes he tarried at the party last night. She supposed he probably knew some things about hangovers. She took the glass and sniffed at its contents, then recoiled in disgust.

"Jesus Christ. What *is* this? It smells like sweat and dirty feet."

"Just hold your nose and drink it. Then hop in the shower. I've got a nice, hot breakfast waiting for you downstairs."

Diz looked up at her. How was it possible for anyone to look so goddamn gorgeous in the morning? She'd shed her jacket, and was standing there in her skirt and un-tucked silk blouse.

"What are you still doing here?"

Clarissa shrugged. "I fell asleep. By the time I woke up, it didn't make sense to leave. Besides," she folded her arms, "I was worried about you."

"You were worried about me?"

Clarissa rolled her eyes. "Yes. I was afraid you might fall out of bed and drown in a pool of your own vomit."

Diz had to smile at that. "I *can* be pretty charming."

"I'm starting to figure that out," Clarissa said, drily.

Diz tried to wink at her, but the action made her head hurt. She raised a hand and rubbed the back of her neck.

"Just kill me now and get it over with," she said.

"You'll be fine." Clarissa nodded at the beverage. "Drink up."

Diz took a deep breath. "Bottoms up," she said, and drained the glass. Five seconds later, she wasn't sure if she wanted to die, or vomit, and then die.

"What the fuck was in that?" she rasped when she could find her voice. "Tar?"

Clarissa just smiled at her. "Shower now. Then come downstairs and eat something." She took the empty glass from Diz, turned around, picked up her shoes, and left the room.

Diz watched her go in amazement. Was any of this really happening? Clarissa actually seemed to be enjoying her little June Cleaver routine.

Of course, June Cleaver never looked quite that hot . . .

Whatever. Diz pushed the blanket aside and slowly got to her feet. So far so good. At least the room wasn't spinning. She made her way to the bathroom and looked at her reflection in the mirror.

Oh, Jesus Christ, she thought. Her eyes looked like a page from Google Maps, and her hair made Don King's look tame. Rachel Maddow could sue her for character defamation and win in a walk. Maybe Clarissa was right, and a shower would help.

She sure as shit hoped so.

In fact, the shower helped a lot. So did putting on some clean clothes. By the time Diz ventured back downstairs, she felt almost human again.

Clarissa had plugged in the lights on the Christmas tree. Diz always got a live tree, and this one was a beauty—a big Frasier Fir, trucked all the way in from the mountains of North Carolina. It was an eight-footer, and it proudly monopolized one corner of the big living room. The tree was decorated with blue and white lights, and hundreds of tiny paper ravens. It had taken her years to fold all the origami birds. It was something she started doing one late night in the stacks of the graduate library—a simple diversion to keep her awake while she drank from her thermos of coffee and tried to ignore the fact that she'd somehow have to show up for work in a few more hours. Year after year, her flock of ravens grew larger, and Diz bought bigger and bigger trees to accommodate them all. She vowed that when she finally finished her Ph.D., she'd stop folding ravens and add a cardinal to the mix—a bright and colorful period to end the longest, run-on sentence of her adult life.

Diz loved Christmas. Not a lot of people knew that about her.

There was music playing. Jazz. It sounded like Sophie Millman. Diz was impressed that Clarissa had figured out how to turn on her sound system. Usually she had to ferret out the goddamn instruction manual whenever she wanted to play it. Diz wasn't all that great with machines. She really belonged in another century. Well. All except for that whole wardrobe thing. Her friends all liked to tease her about how technically savvy she *wasn't*. She didn't even have an iPod. And shit . . . these days, most people had more iPods than they had chromosomes.

That was probably a good essay topic. Maybe she'd tackle that one after she finished writing her dissertation? Why not? Her company published *Wired* magazine. Maybe Clarissa could help her get an article placed?

Clarissa.

Diz still couldn't believe that she was here. She couldn't believe that any of last night had actually happened. She really wanted to ask Clarissa about how much of what she *thought* she recalled was real, but she felt ridiculous about doing so. Besides, if any of it had really happened, Clarissa probably just wanted to forget about it. Diz would only make it worse for both of them if she brought it up.

It was typical, she thought. She'd had the greatest night of her life with the woman who fueled most of her fantasies, and she was too drunk to be able to remember any it with certainty.

Of course, she thought, *if she'd been sober, none of it would have happened in the first place.*

It was a paradox. Like the rest of her life.

She crossed her living room and went into the kitchen. Clarissa was nowhere in evidence, but her small pub table was neatly set for two. And something smelled great. So. It appeared that Clarissa could cook, too. Diz smiled. The cranky redhead was now two-for-two in the June Cleaver Derby.

But where in the hell was she?

There were a finite number of places to look.

She was either out back in the small courtyard that masqueraded as a yard, or she'd somehow managed to make her way to Diz's study.

Nothing much doing in there, Diz thought. Unless, of course, you were into perusing your weight in extant primary source documents related to the rise of ratiocinative fiction. Somehow she doubted that Clarissa would find that very appealing. It even made *her* ass drag, and she was passionate about the stuff.

There was fresh coffee in the pot on the countertop. Diz poured herself a cup.

"I'm in here," Clarissa called out.

The voice was coming from her study—a small room adjacent to the kitchen.

Diz went in search of her.

Clarissa was sprawled out in her leather chair, reading something. She had a stack of loose-leaf pages piled up on the ottoman at her feet. Diz recognized the open document box on the floor next to her chair.

Oh, god. It was her fucking dissertation.

She sighed and crossed the room. "I see you discovered nature's cure for insomnia?"

Clarissa held up the pages. "You mean this? I don't think so."

"No?" Diz perched on an old oak three-legged stool that sat near her chair.

Clarissa shook her head. "It's mesmerizing. I hope you don't mind?"

Diz shrugged. "If you were bored, you could've just watched The Home Shopping Network." *Or gone home,* she thought. Why was Clarissa still here?

"I wasn't bored. I was curious."

"Curious?" Diz asked. "About what?"

"Climate change," Clarissa said dryly. She added the pages she had been reading to the stack at her feet, then dropped them all into the box on the floor. She looked up at Diz with those smoky gray eyes that always spelled trouble. "What do you think I mean?"

Diz set her cup of coffee down on an end table. "To tell the truth, I don't know what to think about any of this."

"This?" Clarissa asked.

"Yeah." Diz was growing exasperated. "*This.*"

32

She wagged a finger back and forth between them. "Any of it. *All* of it."

Clarissa slid forward on her chair. "You're such a nimrod."

"I'm a nimrod?"

"Yes."

Diz felt like her head was starting to swim again, but it wasn't from her hangover. "Do me a favor, Clar. Don't make me work to figure anything out today. I'm only firing on about half of my cylinders right now."

Clarissa grabbed her by the shirtfront. "Come over here and sit down." She pulled her over to the ottoman.

Diz was afraid to look at her. She had a sneaking suspicion that if she did, she'd give too much away. Either that, or she'd turn into a pillar of salt. It was pretty much even money.

"I'm sorry about what happened last night," she said.

Clarissa was quiet for a minute. "Which part?"

Diz looked up at her. "Take your pick."

In the background, Sophie Millman wrapped up her set, and the next CD in the changer started to play. Strains from "Orinoco Flow" filled up the quiet space between them.

Clarissa turned her head toward the sound. "Is that Enya?"

Diz nodded.

"You're certainly full of surprises," she said.

"Is that good or bad?"

"Does it have to be one or the other?"

Diz shrugged.

"What's the matter?" Clarissa asked.

"I feel ridiculous."

"Why?"

"*Why?*" Diz repeated. "Because I acted like an idiot."

Clarissa looked like she was trying hard not to smile. "You always act like an idiot."

Diz narrowed her eyes. "You *were* here last night, right? I mean, I didn't imagine that part, did I?"

"Oh, no," Clarissa agreed. "I was here, all right."

"And did I or did I not . . . well . . . you know?"

Clarissa looked confused. "Did you or did you not *what?*"

33

"Jesus, Clar." Diz's mortification was increasing.

"Did I or did I not kiss you?"

Clarissa gazed up at the ceiling as she pondered her answer. "No. I remember a fair amount of clumsy, drunken groping on your part, and a few vague murmurings about finding my sweater meat, but I don't remember *that* happening."

Diz felt her heart sink. She looked away to hide the blush she knew was on its way. *So it had all been a drunken fantasy.* And she had just added insult to injury by being stupid enough to confess it. How in the hell would she ever recover from this one?

She felt a warm hand on her thigh. She looked back at Clarissa, who was regarding her with a strange little smile on her face.

"You know, you're actually kind of cute when you're riddled with self doubt."

"Gee. Thanks."

Clarissa sighed. "For someone who's such an expert on detective fiction, you sure manage to miss a lot of big clues."

"What's that supposed to mean?"

"Seriously? You can't figure it out? I thought you were some kind of Rhodes Scholar?"

Diz rolled her eyes. "That wasn't *me*, that was Rachel Maddow."

Clarissa just looked amused.

Diz was now on the other side of exasperated. "You really enjoy fucking with me, don't you?"

Clarissa was studying her with those hypnotic eyes. "I'll admit it's an idea that's been gaining some traction lately."

Diz looked at her in surprise.

A timer went off in the kitchen.

"Come on." Clarissa got to her feet. "Let's get you something to eat."

She left the study and headed into the kitchen.

Diz allowed herself to sit there another minute, marinating in her misery, before she stood up, adjusted her hair shirt, and followed the faint but hopeless trail of red violets that led to the world's most unattainable woman.

* * *

34

Clarissa left right after breakfast.

She said she had some "things to take care of," and that she was meeting Lord Nelson at two o'clock.

But Clarissa had been right, and the food really did make Diz feel better. The bacon and Gruyere quiche with leeks and sun-dried tomatoes was sumptuous. Diz ate two large pieces.

"I didn't know you could cook," she said after her first bite.

Clarissa shrugged. "I do all right."

"All right? This is fabulous."

"Don't give me too much credit. You had all the ingredients."

That was true. Diz liked to cook, too.

Clarissa looked around her kitchen. "This really is a beautiful place."

"I was lucky to find it," Diz said. "The former owners get most of the credit for the improvements."

Clarissa looked at her. "Did they sell it to you furnished, too?"

"Well . . . no."

"I've actually been thinking about moving to a new place."

Diz was surprised. Clarissa lived in one of the most desirable, waterfront areas of Baltimore. Condos in her building went for over a million dollars, easy.

"Why?" she asked.

"I don't know," Clarissa said. "Maybe because I spend my days below street level and my nights in the clouds." She shrugged. "I think I'd prefer to live my life someplace in the middle."

Diz smiled at her. "It does have its advantages."

"In your case? I can only imagine."

Diz narrowed her eyes. "What's that supposed to mean?"

"Well," Clarissa explained, "I'm sure it's a real benefit to only have to stumble down a couple of steps when you feel compelled to vomit on someone's expensive, German sedan. I'd have to take a ten minute elevator ride to enjoy that privilege."

Diz sighed. "Remind me to include that feature in the ad if I ever decide to put this place on the market."

Clarissa smiled and finished her coffee.

Then she glanced at her watch.

"I really do have to go." She gestured at their dishes. "Help me clear this away?"

Diz waved a hand over it. "No. I've got this. Go ahead and take off."

"You sure?"

Diz nodded.

Clarissa stood up, and Diz followed suit. "I'll see you out."

They walked to the front door. Diz helped Clarissa into her jacket.

"I really don't know how to thank you," she said. "Believe it or not, this doesn't really happen very often."

"Really?" Clarissa grabbed hold of her mane of red hair and pulled it free from the collar of her jacket—a cascade of red violets filled up the tiny foyer where they stood. "You don't often have overnight guests?"

Diz was embarrassed. "Well . . . no. But that isn't really what I meant."

"Relax, Casanova. I know what you meant."

"Well." Diz stood there stupidly, staring at her shoes and not really knowing what to say. She felt ridiculous and exposed—like she was trying to get up the nerve to ask the prom queen if she could carry her books to homeroom.

Clarissa sighed.

Diz raised her eyes and looked at her.

Clarissa's expression was unreadable. "I'm sure I'll regret this."

Diz was confused. "Regret what?"

"You wanted to know if you kissed me last night?"

Diz nodded.

"And I told you I didn't remember that happening?"

Diz felt her misery compounding. Why was Clarissa bringing this up again? It was like grinding salt into an open wound.

"But," Clarissa took a step closer—the cloud of red violets moving with her, "what I didn't tell you is that I do remember *this* happening."

Clarissa pushed Diz up against the wall and laid one on her. And it wasn't any kind of tentative, you're-drunk-and-won't-remember-this, experimental kind of kiss, either. It was a full-out, head-on, hands-down, hang-ten, hail Mary, all-over-but-the-shoutin' kind of kiss that left nothing to the imagination. And if Clarissa hadn't had such a good handhold on her forearms, Diz would've slid to the floor and ended up in a pool of red violets on the rug.

"Holy shit," Diz said when she finally came up for air.

"Now I'm really going to be late," Clarissa said. She seemed out of breath, too. "See you tomorrow?"

Tomorrow was Christmas Eve. Diz nodded stupidly.

Clarissa kissed her again—quickly this time—then turned toward the door. She was halfway out, then stopped and faced Diz. "What the hell is your real name, anyway?"

Diz smiled sheepishly. "Maryann."

Clarissa raised an eyebrow. "*Maryann?*"

Diz nodded.

"Christ. Clarissa and Maryann. We sound like a lost episode of *Little House on the Prairie.*"

Diz gave her a cocky grin. "Strange bedfellows?"

"You've certainly got that part right." She walked down the steps toward her waiting car. "I'll call you later."

Diz stood in the doorway and watched her leave. Then she went outside and sat down on the top step. It was cold today. The sliver of sky that was visible above the canopy of trees that lined her street looked bleak. The street was wet. Diz held out a hand. Tiny snowflakes landed on her palm. It looked like it was going to be a white Christmas.

She smiled through her haze of confusion and elation. Nothing about what was happening made any kind of sense.

A cardinal landed on the wrought iron railing that flanked the steps to her row house. Diz and the bright red bird stared at each other through the gauzy curtain of swirling snow.

Last night had been surreal. Today was on the other *side* of surreal. And tomorrow? Tomorrow was Christmas Eve. *Christmas Eve with Clarissa.* She sure never saw *that* one coming. Clarissa was right. Sometimes Diz did miss the biggest clues.

But it didn't really matter because, right now, all the omens in her life were looking good.

She gazed at the bright red bird that continued to perch there staring back at her.

Here he was, impossibly ahead of schedule. A talisman to signify the end of her darkest days—uncannily like the icon at the end of a string of rosary beads.

"Hope is the thing with feathers."

Isn't that what Emily Dickinson said?

She smiled at the crimson metaphor, and extended her hand.

"Hello, gorgeous."

A Christmas Tree
Grows in Baltimore

It was a good, old-fashioned nor'easter.

At least, that's what every TV and radio station in the Chesapeake Bay area had been jawboning about since six o'clock that morning, when Diz finally regained consciousness. The office Christmas party had been the night before, and Diz didn't even remember how she got home. She supposed she had Marty to thank for that. Her stalwart office mate was the only real constant in her life these days—ever since Clarissa had moved on to the greener pastures of the ninth floor editorial suite.

Not that she and Clarissa didn't still "see" each other—they did . . . in all those confusing and noncommittal ways that surrounded a fledgling, non-relationship like translucent layers of bubble wrap. In fact, they both were so well insulated from making any missteps that they didn't move at all—in *any* direction. Not forward. Not backward. Not sideways. Not any ways. They were stuck. Immobilized. Just like bugs in amber.

Diz hated amber. It was one of those annoying fall colors that were supposed to look great on her. Just like topaz. Her birthstone. It sometimes seemed like she was the unhappy victim of a jewel-toned conspiracy.

She felt like crap. She needed Advil and a big, greasy breakfast. It was hard to believe that it had now been a year since the morning after last year's party, when Clarissa played nursemaid to her. She recalled coming home in a similar state that night—but there had been one important difference. Clarissa came home *with* her. And Clarissa had stayed with her, too—in the same bed. Although nothing much happened except some grumbling (on Clarissa's part), and some drunken groping (on Diz's part). The following morning, they had acknowledged their no-longer undeniable attraction to each other—and Clarissa even went on to break off her engagement to her granite-jawed, rich boyfriend, "Dash Riprock."

But that was about it. Here they were, twelve months later, still circling each other like wary dogs in a deserted parking lot. It was unfamiliar terrain for each of them. It was unfamiliar for Diz because she had never had a grown-up relationship with a smart, high-functioning woman before. And it was unfamiliar for Clarissa because she'd never had . . . well . . . *any* kind of relationship with a woman before.

None of that was making Diz feel any better.

But there was one bright spot. Tonight was Christmas Eve, and Clarissa was coming by for a late supper. She had even been the one to suggest it. Diz was stunned when her phone rang late on Friday afternoon and she heard Clarissa's voice on the other end of the line.

"What's going on down there?" she asked, with her customary brusqueness.

Diz sat back in her knock-off Herman Miller chair. "Why do you ask? Don't tell me you can hear the screams of the oppressed all the way up there on the ninth floor."

Clarissa sighed. "No. But the smell of fried cabbage *is* wafting up the elevator shaft and permeating all the cashmere coats up here."

" 'Tis the season," Diz quipped. She thought she could sense Clarissa smiling.

"What are you doing?"

"Right now?" Diz asked. "I'm playing a rousing game of 'Find the Dangling Participle' in the latest searing broadside written by our own Grover Westlake."

Grover wrote a monthly column for *Inside the Beltway*, one of Wylie Magazine Group's flagship publications.

"What's he on the rag about this time?"

"Let's see." Diz tapped on her keyboard and brought her screen back to life. "At this point, he's in the midst of a righteous rant about how developers are being allowed to rape the city by cutting down trees along historic avenues and vacant lots without proper authorization."

"That *is* becoming a pandemic."

"Like you'd even notice from your lavish digs on Boston Street." Clarissa still lived in a high-rise, high-dollar condo overlooking the harbor—although she *had* been looking around for more modest accommodations closer to the magazine offices.

"That's not fair," Clarissa replied. "I drive past trees *every* day.

Sometimes I even lower the window of the limousine so I can get a better look at them."

Diz laughed. "Touché."

"Are you through being an asshole?"

"I can maybe manage for about five minutes. Why?"

"I wanted to ask if you had plans for Christmas Eve."

"Christmas Eve?"

"Yes. *Christmas Eve*—the night before Christmas day. Ring any bells?"

"Oh, a few . . . and all of them good, if memory serves."

There was momentary silence on the line.

"What did you have in mind?" Diz asked. She was afraid to presume anything.

"I was thinking that maybe we could connect for a late supper?"

Diz felt her heart rate tic up a notch.

"I might be able to manage that."

"*Might* be able? Why? Do the twins have to be in before curfew?"

Randi and Ronni were sisters who worked in the mailroom, and Diz's one-time holiday romp with them was now firmly enmeshed in the canon of *Wylie Christmas Folklore*.

Diz sighed. "You're never going to let me forget that, are you?"

"Let's see . . . *No*. I don't think I am."

"I've completely reformed."

"Rachel Maddow will be relieved to hear it."

"Hey . . . is it *my* fault that she looks like me!"

"No. In fact, it's one of your more endearing qualities."

"I have endearing qualities?"

"A few."

Diz sat back in her chair again. "Care to elaborate?"

"Not right now. I might, however, on Monday evening—if you can manage to pencil me in."

Diz looked around for a pencil and saw one poking out beneath a stack of galley proofs. She pulled it out and tapped it against the mouthpiece of her phone.

"Got one right here."

"One what?" Clarissa sounded confused.

"A pencil." Diz turned it sideways so she could read what was embossed on its red barrel. "And this one's a beauty, too—*Schultz's Crab House, An Essex Tradition.*"

Clarissa sighed. "Is it sharpened?"

Diz looked at it. "Nope. It's worn to a perfectly round nub."

"Well, kindly use your nub to scrawl my name on your calendar."

Diz thought about her various nubs. "Messy, but effective. Of course, I will have to take my pants off."

"Pervert."

"I knew you'd be pleased."

"That remains to be seen."

"Yes . . . it does."

Silence again. Diz thought maybe she'd gone too far. It wouldn't be the first time.

"Clar?"

More silence.

"Clar—I'm sorry . . ."

"Don't be. It's one of the things we need to talk about."

Talk about? *That couldn't be good.*

"You're not planning to dump me on Christmas Eve, are you?" Diz asked, with more than a trace of panic.

"Planning to? Not at the moment."

Diz rolled her eyes. "Well, that's something, at least."

"How does eight-thirty sound?"

Diz was planning to have drinks with her neighbor, Mrs. Schröder, who was going to be alone for the holidays this year. But Mrs. Schröder never stayed up much past nightfall, so Diz should be back home in plenty of time.

"I can make that work. Want me to cook something for us?"

"I was hoping you'd offer. With this storm rolling in, the city will probably be in lockdown mode by six o'clock."

Diz smiled. "Just get there—I'll take care of everything else."

"I'm counting on it."

Diz could hear another voice in the background. Someone had walked into Clarissa's office.

"Gotta run," she said. "See you later." She hung up.

Diz sat there holding the phone in her hand like she still had something to say.

It was now three days later, and she still had something to say. A *lot* of somethings, in fact, but they would all have to wait until eight-thirty. One thing was clear: it was time to get off this are-we-or-aren't-we gerbil wheel.

Diz made her unsteady way across the room and slowly opened her blinds to admit one small ray of light at a time. She didn't want to push it. But luck was on her side. The sky was the color of dull pewter, and there was no sun to be seen. She squinted her eyes and peered out.

It was snowing . . . *of course.* The sky was only spitting sporadic, tiny flakes at this point. But they were those nasty little insistent ones that tended to gain in intensity and add up to something truly horrendous. *Great.*

She looked across her square scrap of front yard toward the street. A few of the bare branches on Mrs. Schröder's prized linden tree were already spotted with white. They were vibrating in the wind. A bright red cardinal was clinging to one of the lower limbs. It was hard to tell without her glasses, but Diz thought something about its posture suggested that it was pissed-off, too. It kept fluttering its wings in a futile attempt to shake off the snow.

She just hoped it would still be possible for Clarissa to make it over later. Diz looked up at the sky again. *Of course, if she did make it over, she'd probably have to stay the night.*

Diz smiled.

Things could definitely be worse.

❈ ❈ ❈

It snowed steadily all day. By eleven, there was nearly six inches on the ground. By two, that amount had more than doubled. And the wind whipping in from the bay was making it drift all over the place.

She decided to cook something simple for dinner. If Clarissa arrived at eight-thirty, she'd likely be coming straight from her parents' house—and if memory served, the Wylie's did nothing on a small scale. Clarissa would already have had plenty to eat and drink.

Diz wished she had done her grocery shopping earlier in the day. She practically needed snowshoes for the short walk to Eddie's Market. And the winds made it even harder to trudge along in a straight line. But it had been worth the trip. She had a new recipe for Provençale Tomato and Potato soup that she thought might be just right, and she was pairing that with a fresh loaf of rosemary ciabatta bread and a bottle of Culmen Reserva Rioja.

She didn't need any meat, but she noticed that Eddie's had Ostrowski's bratwurst on sale, so she picked up two pounds of the fat links for Mrs. Schröder.

Of course, that probably meant that Diz would have to *eat* two pounds of bratwurst when she went by there later for cocktails, but that was nothing new. Mrs. Schröder was always trying to feed her.

She was nearly home when her cell phone rang. Diz was afraid to stop walking for very long—the snow was really coming down now. Traffic on St. Paul Street had slowed to a crawl. She ducked beneath a sagging awning and fished her phone out of her coat pocket. It was Marty.

"Hello?"

"Yo, Diz?"

"Yeah."

"Where are you? I just went by your house."

"I'm walking back from Eddie's. I needed some stuff for tonight."

"Tonight?" Marty sounded confused. "What's tonight? I thought you were going next door to the widow's for beer and bangers, or whatever in the hell they call that shit."

"That's this afternoon. Clarissa is coming over tonight for a late supper."

Marty didn't say anything right away. Diz could hear the sound of kids yelling in the background.

"Did you say *late* supper?" he finally asked.

"That's the plan," Diz replied.

"Well," Marty drawled. "I wish you loads of luck with that. At the rate this stuff is coming down, she'll need a damn Snowcat to make it all the way over to your place."

Diz ducked her head out and looked up at the sky.

Big mistake. In about two seconds her face was covered with snowflakes.

"Yeah," she agreed. "It's not looking too good right now."

"Want me to come and get you?"

"Are you still out and about?"

"No. But, believe me, I'll take any excuse I can get to escape from these chipmunks."

Marty had three kids, ages two, four, and five and a half. And his wife was pregnant again. Marty was Jewish, but his wife was a former Franciscan nun who seemed determined to atone for her apostasy by populating the planet with little Catholics.

Diz called her "Sister Sheila."

She called Diz "asshole."

They had an understanding.

Diz ducked back beneath her awning. "Thanks for the offer, but I only have a few blocks to go. I'd be home by the time you got the van out."

"Well, if you change your mind, just give me a holler."

"Thanks, man. Hey? Why were you looking for me in the first place?"

"Oh . . . yeah. I was out picking up some extra lights for the Christmas tree. Simon and Teddy pulled the whole goddamn thing over fighting to reach a candy cane and blew half the strands out. Goddamn cheap shit is all made in China these days. I had to put the fucking tire chains on and drive to six damn drug stores before I could find enough replacements. Sheila kept yelling at me to find the starter bulb, but that's like trying to find the verb in a sentence written by George W. Bush."

"So you came by to see if I had any starter bulbs?"

"No. I came by to see if you were still *alive* after last night. You got pretty toasted, girlfriend."

"Whose fault was that? As I recall, you were the one who kept pouring drinks down my throat."

"I know. But you were acting so pathetic it was making *me* sick. You need to get off this damn ledge you've been on with the Duchess for the last year. You should know by now that she's never gonna leave that penthouse and take up with a lowbrow like you."

"I'm hardly a lowbrow, Marty. I have a fucking Ph.D."

"Yeah. And I have a ten-inch dick. What did that get me?"

"Three and a half kids, at last count."

"My point, exactly."

Diz sighed. She knew Marty was right. And with the way things were going, she was pretty sure that Clarissa was coming by to unreel her own version of the same assessment—probably with a lot more profanity, and, hopefully, without a ten-inch dick.

"Okay. I hear you. Let's just see what happens later on, okay?"

"Hey? Give us a call if the Duchess gets snowed-in and can't make it. I'll come and pick you up so you can spend the evening with us."

Diz smiled. "You really are a sweetheart, you know that, Marty?"

"Sweetheart my ass. Alvin's had the shits for the last three days. I'm just looking for somebody else to wipe his ass for one night."

"Gee, thanks."

"What are friends for? Call me later, okay?" He hung up.

Diz shook her head and a cascade of white powder dropped from the brim of her hat like a puff of exhaust. She put her phone away and slapped at the front of her coat to try and clear it off. It was pointless. The snow had reached critical mass. It was in charge now, and there was nothing any of them could do but hunker down and wait for it to run its course.

She stepped back out into the open and began to plod her way along the narrow path that used to be a sidewalk. If she hadn't walked this way so many times before, she'd have no idea where to go. East 31st Street looked unfamiliar. It looked . . . clean. Not like Baltimore at all.

On days like this, she understood the allure ageing Eskimos once were reputed to have for just forgetting about everything and getting lost in a blizzard.

Not today.

She cinched-up her hold on her canvas grocery bag and turned right on Guilford Avenue.

She had promises to keep.

❉ ❉ ❉

48

Christa Schröder was a big, blue-eyed, large-bosomed woman from Königsberg in Bavaria. Her late husband, Karl, moved the family to Baltimore in 1958, when he got a job at Natty Boh—or the National Bohemian brewery. The young immigrant started out by unloading grain trucks in ten-hour shifts, before graduating to the bottling plant. He spent the last fifteen years of his career wrangling Boh's huge copper brew kettles.

Karl Sr. worked for Natty Boh for thirty-one years. In 1970, he moved his wife and son out of their small rented apartment into a spacious rowhouse in the Abell neighborhood of Baltimore. Diz became their neighbor four years ago, when she lucked into the property via a short sale, and now her "Painted Lady" shared a front porch and a scrap of lawn with Christa's.

Karl and Christa had only one son, Karl Jr.—or K2. K2 stayed on in Baltimore and followed in his father's footsteps, going to work for Natty Boh right out of high school. After the company sold out to Stroh and closed its Baltimore operation in 1996, K2 moved with his wife and four children to Eden, North Carolina, to work for Miller/Coors. He came home as often as he could, and his noisy brood was always a fixture next door during the holidays—until this year.

In mid-August, on the hottest day of the summer, the tall, handsome man who had never been sick a day in his life, dropped dead on his front lawn. Christa found him lying at the foot of her prized linden tree, still holding his morning copy of *The Sun* in his right hand.

The twelve-foot linden tree had been a gift from K2, who knew how much his mother missed walking the broad avenues of lighted linden trees during the Weihnachten celebrations in her homeland. Normally, Weihnachten was a joyous holiday for the Schröders. But this year, there was no celebration—no Adventskranz to light, no Tannenbaum, no sweet, spicy Plätzchen or Stollen baking in the kitchen, and no noisy grandchildren sledding out front on the snow-covered street.

Christa was in mourning. K2 had spent three weeks with his mother after his beloved papa was laid to rest in the Immanuel German Lutheran Cemetery on Grindon Avenue—meaning that this year, he would be unable to travel back to Maryland for the holidays.

Diz did her best to try and coerce Christa into at least hanging her Adventskranz, but she refused. The blank windows of her house were unhappy reminders of her great loss. Diz thought the dark, empty house was a like a suburb of her sadness.

Still, Christa was Christa, and when Diz walked over in the late afternoon for a cocktail, she was greeted by a kitchen table loaded with Schnitzel, braised red cabbage, mushroom and mustard Spaetzle, and fried potato Kroketten.

Christa seemed genuinely pleased with the paper-wrapped package of Ostrowski bratwurst, and Diz had to practically arm-wrestle her to prevent her from grilling those up, too.

"I shouldn't even *try* to cook anything for later tonight," she said. "I ought to just ask you for a plate of take-out."

"Ya, well you could do that," Christa said. She piled another tripod of the crispy Kroketten on Diz's plate. "Who is this coming tonight?"

Diz bit into another one of the golden Kroketten. The hot, mashed potato filling was flavored with green onion and nutmeg.

"Clarissa," Diz replied between bites.

"Oh." Christa waved a hand. "That schmissig redhead with the Italienisch car?"

Diz nodded.

"Ya, you watch out for that one, missy."

"What is that supposed to mean?"

"You know."

"No, I don't."

Christa wagged a finger at her. "She is not like you. Not *Lesbierin*."

Diz shrugged. "So?"

"So?" Christa rolled her blue eyes. "*Sheesh.* You kids are all alike these days. All wise guys. All know-it-alls. So what if something shreds your insides—you don't care. You just go for it and damn the consequences."

"Is that really what you think?"

"Ya. You are just like Karl—he never listened to us, either. And he ended up getting his pickle stuck in a wad."

Diz narrowed her eyes. "His what?"

"You know what I mean."

50

"Are you talking about Maisy?" Maisy was Karl's wife.

"Ya. That *cow*."

"I thought you liked Maisy?" Diz was confused.

Christa threw up a hand. "She is all right, now. But Karl was a pig head, and he jumped at the first Mädchen who shook her fanny at him. *You* are just the same as him."

"No, I'm not," Diz protested. "I jump at *every* Mädchen who shakes her tail at me."

Christa glowered at her and shook her white head. "You just be careful."

"I'm trying. But Clarissa is different."

"Ya . . . you all say that. Then you wake up one morning with four kids and no job. So you have to move to someplace awful like Carolina."

Diz wasn't sure how to reply to that.

The wind was picking up. Outside Christa's kitchen window, Diz could see that the streetlight on the corner had come on. She glanced at the wall clock near the doorway that led to the dining room. It was only three-thirty. *Jesus.*

"K2 would be here if he could," she said, softly.

"I know." Christa pushed her own plate away. She had eaten very little. "I don't blame him. Look at my house . . . it's not a place for kids this year."

"We could change that," Diz suggested, hopefully. "I could help you put up the tree and lights."

Karl and Christa always put their tree up on Christmas Eve, in accordance with German tradition. Diz remembered how Karl Sr. would drive every year to a tree farm near Sykesville to cut his own Frasier Fir. For a moment, Diz thought Christa might go along with the idea. She turned her head and stared at the snow drifting against her windowpanes. When she looked back at Diz, her blue eyes were full of sadness.

"No. It's better this way."

"*Why* is it better?" Diz persisted. "Karl would want you to be happy—and you love Weihnachten. It's a time to be joyful, and to celebrate all the good things in life."

Christa pushed back her chair and started collecting their plates. "Not for me. Not this year."

Diz started to protest, but Christa held up a palm to stop her. "One day soon enough, you, too, will know such loss. Right now for me, Advent only means the passing of another week without Karl. There are not enough tree lights in this city to erase that darkness."

Diz found it hard to respond to that.

"Okay," she said, sadly.

"Now," Christa said. "Let's fix your skinny heiress some food, then have a Schnapps before you go."

Diz sighed and got up. She wasn't sure how well-braised red cabbage would go with her Provençale soup, but she knew it would be futile to argue. She picked up a platter of pork Schnitzel and hoped that the rest of Christa's prediction would be a long time coming true.

❋ ❋ ❋

The soup was simmering on the stove, and it smelled wonderful.

The wine was decanted. And Diz had set a small table for them in the living room, so they could see the Christmas tree. The big, live tree was a beauty. Her paper ravens were all there, of course, but this year she'd added white lights to the blue LEDs, a tribute to her nearly completed doctorate in American Literature. Her prelims were over, and her dissertation adviser was reading the final draft of her magnum opus on Edgar Allan Poe before turning it over to the committee for review. Then she would sit for her dissertation defense, and that would be that.

She finished stacking the kindling and logs and stood back to survey the room.

The blue and white lights on the tree looked almost neon.

It looks like a Greek restaurant exploded in here, she thought.

Still, she liked the cool tones of the colors. They went perfectly with the storm that was still raging outside. She'd heard on the news earlier that several neighborhoods in the city had lost power. *God. What a nightmare on Christmas Eve.*

She tried to imagine all those mothers and fathers, arguing in whispers while their kids slept upstairs and they tried to assemble bicycles and dollhouses by flashlight.

Who was she kidding? Kids didn't get stuff like that now. Kids got iPads and video games. Kids got flat panel TVs and cell phones that could program a space shuttle. Kids got whatever-in-the-hell things they screamed for the loudest—and whatever would be guaranteed to keep them quiet and isolated from the rest of corporeal humankind.

Progress. The de-socialization of America carried out via social media. It was an ironic paradox for future Ph.D. candidates to unravel.

Her phone rang. Diz glanced at her watch. Eight-fifteen. Her heart sank. She knew before she picked it up whose voice would be on the other end of the line.

"Diz?"

Yep. It was Clarissa.

"Yeah."

"I have some bad news." At least she sounded genuinely distressed—even out of breath.

"What is it?" Diz was trying not to come unhinged.

"I've been trying to get my car out for the last half hour, and it's not happening. The snow has drifted across the exit to the parking garage."

"Where are you?" Diz asked.

"I'm at my father's condo." Diz could hear talking in the background. "I even tried to talk him into lending me his Tahoe, but he refused." She paused. "Truthfully, I don't think we could even get *that* out. There must be two feet of snow piled up out there. Nobody is going anyplace."

Diz nodded, but didn't say anything.

"Diz?" Clarissa lowered her voice. "Diz . . . honey? I'm really sorry. *I tried.* I want to be there with you—believe me."

"I believe you." What else could she say? It had been nothing but a colossal delusion for her to believe that Clarissa would actually make it over there. This was a blizzard, for Christ's sake.

"Your father is right. You need to stay in and stay safe—it really is too dangerous to travel right now."

She could hear Clarissa sigh. "What will you do?"

Diz looked around her living room, and at the table set for two.

"I'll probably just watch something depressing on TV and go to bed." When Clarissa didn't reply, she added, "I'm kidding. I'll be *fine*. Marty invited me over earlier, so I may hitch up the dog sled and head over there."

"You can *walk* to Marty's?" Clarissa sounded dubious.

"Sure. It's only about three blocks from here."

"Okay." Another pause. "Did you already cook?"

"Yeah. But it's fine—just soup. I can save it. Besides, Mrs. Schröder fed me enough earlier to last until spring."

"The widow next door?"

"That's the one."

"Is her family in town?"

"No. Not this year. Her son couldn't make it back up here since he took so much time off after his father's funeral."

"Well, I'm glad she has you, then."

"Yeah ... I'm a real barrel of laughs."

"Diz ..."

"It's okay, Clar. Really. No worries, all right?"

"Do you mean that?"

"Yes," Diz lied.

More silence.

"Call me in the morning?" Clarissa sounded like a little girl.

"Of course," Diz said with false bravado.

"All right. Goodnight, then."

Diz closed her eyes. "Goodnight."

She started to lower the handset when she heard Clarissa's voice again.

"Diz? I wanted to say that I ... well." She paused. "Merry Christmas, Diz."

Diz nodded and swallowed hard. "You, too."

Clarissa disconnected. Diz stood there, still feeling the vibration of her last words against her ear.

Yeah. She looked at the phone. *Merry fucking Christmas to me.* She wanted to throw the damn thing across the room. But she didn't. She set it down gently, walked to the small dining table, and retrieved the

54

decanter of wine and a glass. She carried them both across the room and plopped down into a leather chair near her neon-lighted tree. After she'd poured herself a big glass of the dark red liquid, she held it up in front of her face to examine it against the backlight of the Christmas tree.

It looked like blood. *Nice.*

She took a big swig.

This sucked candy canes.

She stared up at her tree. A hundred black ravens stared back at her. She could almost hear their silent chorus of *Nevermore!*

She felt like a schmuck for getting her hopes up. They were in the middle of Baltimore's biggest snowstorm in a decade, and *still* she managed to cling to the thin delusion that Clarissa would find a way to join her for Christmas Eve.

She should've taken Christa Schröder's words to heart: *not this year.*

Not any other year, either, apparently.

She thought again about Christa. It was wrong for her to sit over there alone in the dark with only her sadness to keep her company. *Not on Christmas Eve.*

An idea occurred to her.

She put her wine glass down and got up to go into the kitchen to turn off the stove. Then she walked to her hall closet to get her coat and boots.

She might not be able to remedy her own pathetic situation, but she sure as shit could do something about Christa's.

Marty looked stunned when he opened his big front door and saw her standing there in a swirl of snow.

"What the hell are you doing out there?" he asked. He swung the door open wider and grabbed her by the arm. "Get in here before we let all the heat out."

"Who is it?" someone hollered from inside. The level of exasperation in the voice was hard to mistake.

Sister Sheila . . . *of course.*

And now she was yelling again. "Alvin! Stop pulling the dog's tail!"

Diz could hear a TV blasting some place in the back of the house. How was it possible that their kids were still up? It had to be after nine o'clock. It had taken Diz more than half an hour to make her way to Marty's house. She finally gave up on trying to *find* the sidewalks and just trudged along down the centers of the streets. Why not? It wasn't like there was any traffic to speak of.

"Are your kids still awake?" she asked Marty, after she stepped inside, and he pushed the door closed behind her.

He rolled his eyes. "You're kidding me, right? They don't *ever* sleep."

"Jeez, Marty."

"What are you *doing* out in this mess? Where's the Duchess?"

"At her father's. She couldn't get out."

"Yeah? I'm not surprised. It's nasty out there."

"Who is it, Marty?" Sheila asked again.

"Diz," he called back.

"Diz?" Sheila answered with surprise. "Well tell her to get in here and grab a kid."

Diz felt the floor vibrating and a big, black and white Siberian Husky bolted into the foyer and skidded to a stop at her feet. It had something in its mouth.

When Marty realized what the dog was carrying, he tried to grab it away from her. "Sadie! Drop! *Drop it!*" Sadie was doing a masterful job dodging Marty's lunging hands. "Jesus, Sadie . . . *give me that damn diaper.*"

Sadie glanced up at Diz with her clear blue eyes, before she sensed a threat and whipped her head to the side. Simon and Teddy were thundering toward her on their fat little legs. In an instant, she was off like a shot—her trophy still intact.

The two marauding boys roared through the foyer and continued after her without stopping.

"Don't run in the house!" Marty yelled after them.

In the living room, Alvin was screaming, "Sadie took my didie!"

Marty sighed and ran a hand over his face.

"Sorry. It's been a rough night."

"No problem. Look, man, I'm here because I need a favor."

56

"A favor?" He looked suspicious. "What is it?"

"I need to borrow your van."

"My van? Tonight?"

Diz nodded.

"Are you *nuts?*" he asked.

She shrugged. "I wouldn't ask, Marty, if it wasn't really important."

"What are you going to do? Go and try to get her?"

"Her? Her who? Clarissa?"

He nodded.

"No. This doesn't have anything to do with Clarissa."

He looked dubious.

Diz held up a hand. "I swear. It's not about her at all. It's something else—something I need to do for somebody who's all alone."

"I don't get it. Why does it have to happen tonight? In case you didn't notice," he jerked a thumb toward the front door, "there's a blizzard out there."

Diz sighed. "I realize that. But didn't you say earlier that you had your tire chains on?"

"Yeah . . ."

"Then I should be fine. I don't have far to go."

He hesitated.

"Come on, man. I wouldn't ask if it wasn't really important."

He sighed. "Sheila will have my ass if she finds out."

"Sheila already *has* your ass, Marty."

"True." He opened the hall closet and got out his coat. "I'll be right back," he called out.

"Where are you going?" Sheila asked.

"I'm walking Diz out. I'll be right back."

"Oh, god, Alvin . . . *not on the couch, again!*" Sheila sounded like she was about to come unhinged. "Marty!"

Marty turned to Diz. "Let's go before she has a chance to come out here make you take Alvin along with you."

Diz pulled open the big front door. "You don't have to ask me twice."

They made their way to Marty's driveway. Fortunately, his prized "Inferno Red" Dodge Caravan was backed into its space. He grabbed a snow shovel and broom that were leaning up against the porch, and tossed the broom to Diz. While Marty shoveled snow, Diz used the broom to sweep off the windshield. Once they had broken up the worst of the drift across his driveway, he pulled something out of his pocket and walked around to the driver's side door.

"Get in—I need to show you a few things."

"Marty . . . I know how to drive."

"Not this thing, you don't. It's special."

"Special?"

He nodded. "Trust me."

Marty fiddled with the door lock, then climbed inside and unlocked the passenger door for Diz.

"Okay," Diz said with impatience. "What is it that you have to show me?"

Marty reached inside a two-toned bowling shoe that sat on the center console between the front seats. He held up a short-barreled flathead screwdriver. "How to start it, for one thing."

"A *screwdriver?*" Diz asked.

He nodded.

"Did you lose your keys?" she asked.

"Never had keys to lose," he said. He shoved the screwdriver into the ignition and angled it so it would connect with the starter. "You have to hold it at exactly this angle, or it won't work."

"Are you kidding me with this? Where did you get this thing? Midnight Auto Supply?"

He looked at her. "*No.* For your information, I got it from some guy in Michigan."

"*Some guy?* Did he also sell you a Rolex?"

Marty sat back against the high-backed leather seat. "Do you want to use my ride, or not?"

Diz sighed. "Go ahead. I'm listening."

"Okay." Marty turned the screwdriver, and the engine roared to life. The cabin was immediately filled with loud, soulful music."

"What the hell is that?" Diz shouted above the noise.

Marty looked at her. "*Holding Back the Years.* Classic 80s."

Diz rolled her eyes. "I got that part. Can you turn it down?"

He shook his head. "This Simply Red CD was stuck in the changer when I bought the van. You can't turn it down, or off . . . or eject it."

Diz was horrified. "You mean it always plays . . . and this loud?"

He nodded again. "After a while, you get used to it." He was tapping his fingers on the top of the steering wheel. "Great lyrics."

"No wonder your kids are insane," Diz muttered.

"What did you say?" Marty asked.

She looked at him. "I said I bet the kids love it."

He nodded. "It puts Alvin right to sleep. Sometimes Sheila just drives him around the neighborhood to get him to punch out."

Diz sighed. "So . . ." She picked up the shoe from the center console. It was also full of loose change. "Are there any other special features I need to know about?"

Marty was admiring the shoe. "That's a beauty, isn't it? It came with the van. It's part of the Calvin Klein package." He sighed. "Too bad they don't fit Sheila."

"Calvin Klein?" Diz examined the smooth-soled shoe.

Marty pointed toward the heel cup. "Yeah. See?"

Diz looked at it more closely. The initials "CK" were plainly visible. She lowered the shoe and looked at her friend. "Marty . . . believe me. Calvin Klein *never* designed bowling shoes."

"He didn't?"

Diz shook her head. "Where did you get this thing, exactly?"

He shrugged. "In the parking lot at Thunderbowl Lanes in Allen Park. Sheila and I went out there for the PBA World Series of Bowling." His eyes looked dreamy. "It was *fine*."

"Where the hell is Allen Park?"

Marty held up his hand and pointed at the base of his thumb. "It's right about here—not too far from Detroit."

"You bought a stolen van?"

"Hey?" He shrugged. "It was only eighteen-hundred bucks—and we have *three* kids." He rolled his eyes. "Soon to be four."

Diz laughed. "I guess it was a pretty good trip."

"No shit. My cousin, Murray, works for the MVA. He fixed it."

"Fixed what? The no-title thing?"

"That, and the fact that the VIN number was filed off."

Mick Hucknall had finished holding back his years, and was now crooning about opening up a red box. The passenger compartment was warming up nicely. Diz glanced over her shoulder. The back seat was choked with car seats. Behind it, the van looked like it was full of boxes and bags.

"Anything else I need to know?" Diz asked.

"Just this." Marty handed her a mini-Leatherman tool.

Diz took it. "Do I want to know what this is for?"

"You use the nail file to unlock the driver's side door. It works like a charm."

"Right."

"Don't worry that the thing runs kinda loud—the catalytic converter got punched out."

Diz gestured toward the CD changer in the dashboard. "Who would notice?"

"Good point." Marty put his hand on the door handle. "That's about it. Anything else you need—just give me a call."

Diz nodded.

Marty climbed out. "Keep that Leatherman in your pocket. The doors lock automatically when you get out. Once Sheila locked Simon and Teddy in here with Sadie, and they were stuck for three and a half hours." He shook his head. "I'm still not sure it was an accident."

Diz smiled at him. "You're a prince, Marty. I won't be gone for long—I promise."

He stood back while she climbed across the console and got into the driver's seat.

"See you in a bit," she said.

Marty closed the door and waved at her as she slowly pulled out onto the snowy street.

❊   ❊   ❊

After four tries, Diz lucked out and found a twenty-four-hour CVS on North Charles Street that was still open. It even looked like someone had plowed a single lane up into its parking lot.

She pulled in and stopped—leaving the flashers going on the van so nobody would think it was stuck or broken down and tow it off.

The inside of the store looked like it had been ransacked. The shelves were mostly empty, except for a few strands of synthetic garland in garish colors and some random boxes of mismatched Christmas cards. Oh . . . and a five-foot, inflatable Hello Kitty in a Santa hat.

But there were no Christmas tree lights and no ornaments. Anyplace.

But she had to admit that the hip hop rendition of "Millie Pulled a Pistol on Santa" that was playing on the store's sound system sounded pretty good after thirty minutes of being hammered by blaring Simply Red tunes.

Only two people appeared to be working. A cranky-looking man in the pharmacy at the back of the store did his best to ignore her. The third time she cleared her throat, he looked up from behind his wall of pills and stared at her.

"Excuse me . . . I'm looking for Christmas tree lights?" she said.

He grunted at her and pointed toward the front of the store.

She looked toward the area he appeared to be indicating.

"I looked on the shelves—they're pretty empty," she said.

He threw up his hands and shrugged.

She took a deep breath and tried again. "I was wondering if you had some in the back, or maybe someplace else in the store?"

He glared at her. "You'll have to ask Tyrone." He pointed again. "Up front."

She bit back an expletive. "*Thanks.* Merry Christmas."

He grunted and dropped his eyes back to his bottles of pills.

Diz made her squishy way back up to the front of the store. There were muddy-looking puddles all over the place. It was clear that this particular store had seen a lot of business tonight.

Tyrone was camped out on a stool behind the front counter, flipping through a copy of *Soap Opera Digest.* He sat up straight and tried to conceal it as Diz approached, and she pretended not to notice, but she *was* surprised to discover that Lynn Herring was returning to *General Hospital.*

"Hello," she said to Tyrone. "The terribly accommodating and friendly man in the pharmacy said I should ask you about locating some Christmas tree lights?"

"We don't have any more," he said, without emotion.

"Not *any?*" Diz asked. "Not in the back—or maybe in another section of the store? I don't even care what *kind* they are, as long as they light up."

He thought about that. Then he reached beneath the counter and hauled up a bulging, white plastic bag with a bright red CVS logo emblazoned on its side. "We have *these.* Some lady just returned them all—said they were the wrong kind."

"Do they work?"

He shrugged. "I think so. She just said they were the wrong kind."

"I'll take them."

"They're outdoor lights," he said.

Diz was digging out her wallet. "Fine."

"They're LEDs," he added. "*Expensive* ones."

"I don't care."

"They're pink."

Diz hesitated. *Pink?* She looked at Tyrone.

He shrugged. "Take 'em or leave 'em, lady. They're all we got."

She sighed. "Okay." She handed him her credit card.

"That'll be eighty-two-fifty."

"Eighty-two-fifty? Are you *kidding* me? What the hell are they made out of? Waterford Crystal?"

"You want 'em or not?"

"Yeah. All right. Just ring it up, okay?"

He swiped her card and handed her the bag. Diz was shocked at how heavy it was. She figured there must be ten thousand lights in it. Correction. Ten thousand *pink* lights.

Great.

Oh well, it's the thought that counts, right?

She took her bag and waded back out to Marty's van. The nail file on the Leatherman worked like a charm. Thankfully, so did the tire chains. In two minutes, she was back out on North Charles Street, headed for the nearest—still open—tree lot. She remembered seeing a baker's dozen of the little mom & pop stands all along some of the major city avenues, but it was now nine forty-five on Christmas Eve, and there was more than twenty inches of snow on the ground. The first five lots she passed were already closed—and woefully bereft of trees. She knew better than to try and navigate off any of the main thoroughfares—even the main city drags were down to one open lane (if you could call them that) in each direction.

In desperation, she made a U-turn and drove south on Charles Street toward the Inner Harbor. The winds blowing in off the bay in this area were causing the snow to drift even more dramatically. No wonder Clarissa wasn't able to get out. The going got rougher and rougher, and there were fewer and fewer cars down here. Just when she was about to give up, she saw the hazy outline of a string of naked light bulbs stretched across what looked like a vacant city lot. When she drew closer, she could read the hand-lettered sign: "Otis Campbell Fresh Cut."

Eureka! It was a tree stand . . . or what appeared to be left of one. And wonder of wonders, it was *still* open. At least, she thought it was, since all the lights were still on. She maneuvered the van over and pulled off the road into the small lot. She could see all the standard cutting and netting gizmos next to some saw horses beneath a shelter and a few scraggly-looking wreaths tacked up on some pegboard. Everything else was covered with snow. Unfortunately for her, there didn't appear to be any trees left—not unless you counted the big one leaning against the side of a beat-up Shasta trailer. Its branches were sagging beneath the weight of all the snow, but it looked pretty decent—like maybe it was some kind of balsam fir? It was hard to tell, and right now, she wasn't inclined to be picky. Lights glowed inside the trailer, so she turned off her engine and hopped out to make her way over and investigate. The quiet outside stopped her dead in her tracks. She didn't think she'd ever not heard Baltimore quite like this. She even thought she could hear the flakes hitting the arms of her coat.

Of course, even I-95 during rush hour would seem quiet compared to the interior of Marty's van. Her head was actually reeling from the incessant pounding it had been taking for the past hour. She glanced at the "Inferno Red" van.

So much for your Calvin Klein editions . . .

63

God. It was cold as shit down here. But the snow actually seemed like it was starting to lighten up a bit. The flakes were big and fluffy now—the fat, fairy tale kind that clung so beautifully to everything in Bing Crosby movies, or that festooned the cheap, Currier & Ives dinnerware her parents had when she was growing up.

When Diz got closer to the trailer, she could make out the muffled sound of a TV coming from inside. The little camper was nearly buried in the snow—the drifts nearly reached the bottoms of the windows. Blue light flickered behind flimsy-looking café curtains.

There was a beat-to-shit pickup pulled up next to the trailer. Its bed was weighted down with firewood and snow, and there were no visible tire tracks in evidence. It was clear that the vehicle hadn't been moved in a while.

She wondered why any thinking person would be holed-up in this tin can during a blizzard?

Beside the two-toned door of the trailer was a banged-up aluminum trashcan. The lid was askew, and Diz could see discarded pizza boxes and empty liquor bottles piled up inside it. She squinted her eyes. Aristocrat Vodka. *Nice.*

Okay. Maybe it *wasn't* so hard to understand how somebody could be holed-up out here during a blizzard.

Against her better judgment, she rapped on the aluminum door.

"Who is it?" a man inside barked.

Her instinct was to turn around and head back to the safe haven of Simply Red. But she'd come this far, so why not try to finish the deed? She tightened her hold on the mini-Leatherman.

"Are you still open?" she called out.

She could hear someone's feet hit the floor. The tiny trailer shook with each heavy footstep.

"Hold your fucking horses," the voice inside growled.

Diz took a step backward, ready to beat as hasty a retreat as the snowpack would allow.

The door to the trailer was thrown open, and an enormous, red-headed man wearing a buffalo plaid shirt filled up the opening.

"I'm outta trees, lady—sold the last one two hours ago. All I got left is a couple of those wreaths." He pointed a meaty hand toward the pegboard beneath the makeshift shelter. "I can make you a good deal on all of those. Cash only," he added.

Diz sighed. "I've been all over the city, and this is the only lot I've found that's even still open. I was just hoping that maybe you had something left over."

He was looking at her strangely. "Nope. Why'd you wait so late to go looking?"

"It's complicated."

He shifted his weight, and the trailer shook again.

"You're that yakky woman from TV, aren't you?" he asked.

Diz sighed, and was about to correct him when she got an idea.

"You recognize me?" she asked, innocently.

He nodded. "I don't really watch those liberal channels, but I seen you from time to time."

She smiled and pushed up her horn-rimmed glasses. "I'm on assignment, doing a special on Christmas in Baltimore tonight. So, you're a small business owner? How's that working out for you?"

"We get screwed," he added.

"Are you Mr. Campbell?" she asked.

He nodded.

"How long have you been running this tree stand?"

"About six years. I had to move down here from Towson. Goddamn local commies wouldn't let me park my camper on the lot."

She shook her head. "Pathetic."

"No shit. All I'm trying to do is make an honest living. I don't mooch off the system like the rest of those lazy bastards. All they want is the next fucking handout."

Diz egged him on. "What do you think about healthcare reform, Mr. Campbell?"

He turned purple. "Fucking socialists wanna ruin this country. I don't need any goddamn handout from the commie feds ... when I get sick, I go to the emergency room, and they fix me up for fifteen bucks. What's wrong with *that?* But, no. Some people just want to be taken care of like the world owes them something."

"Mr. Campbell, I think we're letting all your heat out."

He looked over his shoulder.

"Lemme get my boots, and I'll come out there."

"I don't want you to miss your program." The TV was still going in the background.

He waved a hand dismissively. "It's just an old movie—more commercials than anything."

"What is it?"

Otis rumbled his way across the inside of tiny trailer.

"Damn channel's been running this thing all week. It's some old black and white about kids in New York City. It's the only station I get out here without cable." He returned with a muddy pair of black arctic boots. "Their dad was some kind of Irish cop."

Diz glanced at his tiny TV. Dorothy McGuire was giving Lloyd Nolan her best full-screen, earnest look.

"*A Tree Grows in Brooklyn?*" she asked.

He grunted. "Somethin' like that." He sat down on a rust-colored recliner to pull on his overshoes. "It's kind of a chick flick."

"I notice that you have one tree left out here," she said, jerking her thumb toward the big fir. "The one that's leaning up against your trailer."

"Yeah. I can't sell that one." He reached over to an aluminum TV table that sat next to his chair and picked up a glass that was half full of clear liquid. He tipped it up and drained it. "The trunk is cracked in the middle."

"It looks pretty sturdy," she suggested.

"No way, lady. I know your game . . . I sell it to you, then when it breaks in half and crushes your goddamn plasma TV, you and your high-priced trial lawyer buddies will try to *sue* my ass. Then I'll be tomorrow night's headline on your commie news channel." He emitted a redolent belch. It hovered in the stale air like a period to his sentence.

Diz started to protest when light from a pair of headlights blazed across the side of the trailer. Another car was crunching its way into the lot. She turned around. It was a cab.

A cab? Tonight?

"Jesus fucking Christ," Otis Campbell complained. "Who's here now? Walter Cronkite?"

He stomped to the opening and stepped down out of the trailer, and slammed the door behind him. An avalanche of snow slid off its roof and landed on the back of his head.

It did *not* improve his mood.

The cab pulled to a stop next to Marty's van. It was a bright yellow and lime green AMC Eagle, decked out with a lift kit and spinners. A magnetic sign attached to the driver's side door side proclaimed "Beaver Cab Co.—Best Dam Ride in Town." The falling snow made crazy patterns inside the bright, narrow beams of its headlights.

Somebody was getting out. It was a woman. She had a head of thick, auburn hair.

Diz felt her stomach lurch.

Clarissa? *Impossible.* It had to be some kind of sick, wish fulfillment. A delusion brought on by the storm, and her festering disappointment.

The apparition started making its way toward them.

"Just what in *holy hell* are you doing out here?" it demanded.

Nope.

It was Clarissa all right. And she was pissed . . . of course.

"What am *I* doing out here?" Diz asked. "What are *you* doing out here?"

Clarissa rolled her eyes. "I was on my way to *your* place." She jerked her thumb toward the four-wheel drive cab. "Do you have any idea how much it cost to find a ride like this?"

Diz looked at what had to be the most eclectic cab she'd ever seen. It still sat there, idling. A big cloud of warm exhaust swirled around it like smoke. She observed that its off-duty light was now illuminated. The windows of the cab were tinted so dark, you couldn't see inside. It could have had a driver—or not. The thing looked like hell's chariot.

Clarissa was talking again. "I noticed that some idiot was stopped over here when we rolled by. It was five minutes later before I realized that the idiot was *you.*"

The cab slowly made its way across the lot and out onto the snowy street. Diz half expected it to take off vertically.

"Nice rims," Otis Campbell muttered.

They both looked at him.

"Look," he said. "Could we just take care of business, here? I'm freezing my ass off. Unless one of two you is interested in a great—*cash*—deal on a wreath, I got a date inside with my TV and a pint of vodka."

Diz took hold of Clarissa's elbow. "Mr. Campbell, I'd like you to meet my producer, Clarissa Wylie."

"Your *what?*" Clarissa looked at her like she'd lost her mind.

"Oh, come on, Clar . . . don't be *shy.*" Diz squeezed her elbow and glared at her. "This nice man has seen our show before—*he recognized me right away.*"

Clarissa was looking at her with narrowed eyes. "Have you been drinking?"

Diz pulled her close and wrapped an arm around her shoulders. "What a great little kidder." She smiled at Otis. "She knows we can't start celebrating until we finish our special little Christmas story."

Clarissa wasn't buying it. "Have you lost what little bit of sense god gave you?"

Diz winked at Otis. "You know how bosses are—always making you work the graveyard shift on holidays."

"Rat bastards." He nodded. "What's that story again?"

Bingo.

"We're doing a piece about Baltimore's . . . um . . . *Scottish* widows, who are all alone on Christmas Eve." Clarissa started to say something, but Diz jerked her into silence. "We've been out all night, trying to find a tree to decorate their community center." She slowly shook her head. "Poor dear, old things."

He looked suspicious. "They have a community center?"

"Oh, yeah," Diz said with confidence. "It's on O'Donnell Street—near the old brewery."

"They don't have a Christmas tree?" he asked.

Diz shook her head. "It's a sad story. All about 'The Superannuated Widows League of Loch Raven,' and how they are among the city's forgotten minority." She lowered her voice. "The Fox News Channel was trying to scoop us, but we got to it first. Now they're running a retrospective on Hillary Clinton's hairdos."

Clarissa cleared her throat. Diz couldn't even *remember* the last time the crusty editor had kept silent this long. She stole a quick look at her, just to make sure she was still breathing. Yep. She was. Diz chalked it up as another Christmas miracle.

Clarissa stared back at her with a unique mixture of amusement and disbelief—a look she held the patent for.

Otis was thinking it over. He glanced at the last tree on his lot—the big one, with the broken trunk.

He burped and wiped his mouth with the back of a hammer fist. Then he sighed. "Okay . . . I'll let you have it."

Diz smiled brightly at him.

"Under *one* condition," he added.

Her smile faded.

"You gotta *catch* it."

"Excuse me?" Diz wasn't sure she'd heard him correctly.

"You know what I'm talking about." He tossed his head toward the small camping trailer. "Just like in that goddamn movie." He chuckled. "I throw it, and if you catch it, it's yours . . . free of charge."

Diz and Clarissa exchanged glances. Then, in tandem, they looked at the tree in question.

It had to be eight feet tall.

And it was weighted down with about two tons of snow.

Clarissa opened her mouth to speak, but Diz cut her off. "Deal."

The big man nodded. "Lemme get some gloves . . . this sucker's gonna be heavy."

He turned around and tromped his way back to the trailer.

As soon as he was out of earshot, Clarissa yanked her arm free. "Have you lost your fucking mind?"

Diz shrugged.

"*Superannuated Widows?*" Clarissa quoted.

Diz smiled. "Like that? Charles Dickens . . ."

"I *know* what it is, thank you very much. Just what in the hell is going on?"

Diz sighed. "Mrs. Schröder is all alone this year. Karl's gone, and K2 can't make it home." She shrugged. "I've been so selfish and self-absorbed, I didn't even notice that she hadn't put up a single Christmas ornament. And Christa *loves* her Weihnachten celebration more than she loves *liverwurst*—which, by the way, you cannot measure with existing technology."

Clarissa actually smiled at that. "So you decided to get her a Christmas tree?"

Diz nodded.

"At ten o'clock on Christmas Eve."

Diz nodded again.

"In the middle of a blizzard."

"Right."

Clarissa sighed. "Why the whole Rachel Maddow routine?"

"Hey . . . don't blame me for that one. He made the mistake—and he was being totally uncooperative about selling me what, arguably, is the last fucking tree in Baltimore. So I went with it. And, in case you haven't noticed, it seems to be working like a charm."

They heard the door to the tiny trailer slam and looked over to see Otis making his way toward them. He was pulling on a pair of work gloves. Diz noticed that he had added something else to his ensemble, too. A bottle of Aristocrat was sticking out of his jacket pocket.

"I'm going to kill you for this," Clarissa hissed, "just as soon as I get out of traction."

"Let's rock and roll." Otis chuckled. "This better make the eleven o'clock news."

He walked over to the big balsam fir, grabbed it by its base, and hauled it upright. Then he gave it a good shake to loosen some of the snow that had accumulated on its boughs. He hauled it away from the trailer and stood facing them from a distance of about twelve feet. The tree topped him by at least eighteen inches.

"You bitches feelin' lucky?"

Clarissa groaned.

"Where do you want us?" Diz asked.

"Right there is good. He gave the tree another shake for good measure. "Remember. You have to *catch* it, or else there's no deal."

"Right," Diz said. She turned toward Clarissa. "Get behind me and turn around. Then plant your feet and push hard against my back. Use *all* of your weight."

"This is insane," Clarissa grumbled. But she did as Diz asked.

70

"Ready?" Otis bellowed. He grabbed hold of the tree with both hands and began to raise it up over his head. He looked like Charles Atlas.

A drunk and sadistically *cranky* Charles Atlas.

Jesus, Diz thought. *We're both going to die.* She had a momentary, panicked desire to whisper, "I love you" to Clarissa. She thought she might not get another chance.

"Ready!" she called out, instead.

Everything that happened next seemed to take place in slow motion. Diz watched Otis gingerly pump the tree up and down a time or two to get his momentum going, then he heaved it up and threw it at them with all the grace of a Highland Scot, going for broke in a caber toss.

The big fir sailed through the air in a hail of snow and frozen boughs. Diz thought she actually could smell the resin leaking from the sticky blisters on its smooth, gray bark as it drew closer. Soon, her entire field of vision filled up with a hazy blur of green and white.

Then it hit her. Head on—like a Mack truck made out of pine needles.

Jesus, Mary, and Joseph!

She'd never felt anything this goddamn heavy. The force of its impact knocked the wind out of her and made her lungs burn. Branches and pine needles stung and scraped her face, and heavy clumps of snow cascaded around her and pushed its way inside her clothing. She staggered to her knees.

She could hear Clarissa groaning. Diz felt herself beginning to slide backwards as Clarissa fought to maintain her footing.

It was ridiculous. But somehow, miraculously, *incredibly,* against all odds, and in a manner that would have made Rachel Maddow proud, she managed to remain upright, hanging on to the monstrous tree.

She could hear laughter. The ringing in her ears made it hard to tell where it was coming from.

She slowly became aware that behind her, Clarissa was chanting something.

"Oh my god, oh my god," she was saying, over and over.

"You did it. You actually *did* it."

Diz spat out a mouthful of pine needles. "*We* did it."

Otis Campbell had made his way over to them. He was still chuckling. "I guess you win."

Diz let go of her stranglehold on the Sasquatch of Christmas trees, and the enormous thing rolled to the ground and landed at his feet with a loud crack.

Diz stared down at it. *You gotta be kidding me?*

The tree lay at her feet in two perfect sections. It had split completely in half—*lengthwise*—just like the temple veil. Her aching shoulders sagged, and she looked forlornly up at Otis.

He shrugged. "I told you it was cracked." He unscrewed the cap from his bottle of vodka and took a drink.

Diz sighed and turned around to help Clarissa scramble back up to her knees.

"What happened?" Clarissa asked.

Diz pointed at their bisected trophy. "It broke."

"It *what?*" Clarissa stared down at the tree in horror. Then she socked Diz on the arm. "*Asshole!* We could've been killed catching that thing."

"Maybe we can salvage part of it?" Diz suggested, hopefully.

Otis was chuckling again.

Clarissa gave him a murderous look. "Don't even *go* there, buddy."

He smirked at her and took another big pull from his pint bottle, before magnanimously offering it to Diz. She was half-tempted to take it from him when she noticed something change in his expression. He lowered his bottle and clutched at his abdomen with his free hand.

"Are you okay, man?" she asked. His color looked bad. It was kind of . . . *green*.

Oh, shit, she thought. *No, no, no . . .*

She used all of her remaining strength to body-slam Clarissa and roll her out of the way.

"Hey!" Clarissa yelled, as they went sprawling, face-first, into a pile of snow. Diz came to rest on top of her a nanosecond before Otis commenced heaving his guts out—all over what was left of their prized balsam fir. His retching went on and on. A miasma of cheap vodka and recycled pizza slowly overwhelmed the scent of fresh cut pine.

Diz and Clarissa untangled themselves and rolled up into sitting positions, slapping at the snow on their clothes.

"That was perfectly *disgusting*," Clarissa said, without a trace of charity.

Diz actually felt sorry for Otis, who was still looking pretty rough.

Their Christmas tree, of course, was now a complete write-off. What remained of Otis's . . . *dinner* . . . was now strewn all over it, steaming in the cold air.

Otis stood upright and wiped his mouth off on the sleeve of his jacket. He looked at the now-defiled tree, then back at the two of them.

He gave Diz a lopsided smile. "Think those widows would like a great deal on a wreath?"

❋ ❋ ❋

"What the hell is up with this music?"

Clarissa knew that Diz was driving Marty's van, so she didn't bat an eyelash at the screwdriver ignition key, but the music blasting at ear splitting decibels was a bridge too far.

"Marty says the CD is stuck in the changer, and you can't turn it off or lower the volume," Diz explained.

Clarissa rolled her eyes. "So he drives around listening to this endless cacophony of Simply Red tunes?"

Diz nodded.

"That explains volumes about Marty."

"What?" Diz didn't hear what she said.

"Oh, for god's sake." Clarissa reached over to the center console and picked up the bowling shoe where Diz had dropped the Leatherman tool. She rummaged around inside it until she found what she was looking for.

"What are you doing?" Diz asked.

"Taking care of a nuisance," she replied. She straightened out a paper clip, then leaned forward and shoved the end of it into a small hole next to the CD door on the radio. When nothing happened, she smacked the end of it with the flat of her hand. There was a brief, whirring sound, and the Simply Red CD ejected.

Clarissa calmly removed it and stashed it behind the sun visor.

The sudden quiet inside the van was surreal.

But that was Clarissa. The woman didn't have a passive bone in her body. If she ran into a problem, she faced it head on. She rarely took no for an answer, and she never took prisoners.

Diz wasn't sure how Marty would take the news. She feared that little Alvin might never sleep again. *Maybe she'd just stick the CD back into the changer before she took the van back?*

They were crawling up North Charles Street. In the ninety minutes since Diz struck out on her goodwill mission, road conditions had deteriorated to the point that the single lanes that had been plowed earlier were now barely passable. There were no other cars on the road—not even rogue members of the Beaver Cab Co. fleet.

Diz felt completely demoralized and beyond disappointed that her desire to do something nice for Christa had failed so miserably. All she had to show for her altruism were aching muscles, wet socks, and a bulging bag loaded with high-dollar pink LED lights.

Well . . . that and a soggy, cold, and extremely pissed-off passenger.

Clarissa didn't ask Diz to take her home. She just climbed into the van and strapped herself in without speaking. After they'd driven for about ten minutes—which was about a mile and a half—Diz decided that she needed to ask Clarissa where she wanted to go.

Clarissa glared at her. "Where do you think?"

"I honestly don't know."

"There appears to be no end to the things you honestly don't know."

Diz looked at her. "Am I supposed to know what that means?"

"Let's break this down into its component elements," Clarissa said with exaggerated patience. "What possible motivation might I have to hi-jack my retirement savings and take a snow-covered death ride in a bilious green hoopty on Christmas Eve?"

Diz thought about it. "You were tired of watching reruns of *A Tree Grows in Brooklyn* on TV?"

"Close, but no cigar."

"You wanted to enjoy the Christmas lights on South Charles Street?"

"It's true that abandoned buildings *are* lovely in the snow . . . but, no."

"Your father ran out of eighty-year-old Scotch?"

Clarissa raised an eyebrow.

"Okay," Diz said with resignation. "I give up."

"That's the problem with you. You *always* give up—and way too soon."

Diz was doing her best to stay focused on the road ahead. It felt safer. "I don't know what to say."

Clarissa sighed. "Well, fortunately for you, I *do*." She laid a hand on Diz's thigh. "I wanted to be with *you*, nimrod. That's why I was willing to risk becoming an organ donor."

"Oh." Diz began to feel slightly woozy. "Okay." She stole a shy look at Clarissa. "Really?"

Clarissa squeezed her thigh. "Yes. Really."

Diz tried to suppress her smile, but failed miserably.

"Are you hungry?"

Clarissa thought about that for a second. "You know, I think I am." She leaned across the console and kissed Diz lightly on the ear. "There's nothing quite like a good old fashioned roll in the snow to get a girl's appetite up."

Red violets. The unmistakable scent that clung to Clarissa like a second skin filled up Diz's world. The van swerved, and Diz fought to keep it going in a straight line.

Guilford Avenue was right ahead. Diz negotiated the turn and slowly drove down her street. The snow had nearly tapered off, but there were still a few fat flurries flying around. Everything in sight was covered in a blanket of pure white. The street was completely quiet. Most of the Painted Lady rowhouses that made up her neighborhood had Christmas lights strung around their porch railings and front doors, giving the street a warm and welcoming glow.

Diz pulled Marty's van to a stop in front of the big house she shared with Christa. It was pointless to try and park it. The snowdrifts were knee-high all through here. The best she could do was get it out of the center of the street.

After they ate some soup, she'd need to return the van to Marty's place. She hoped Clarissa would be willing to stay on with her, and not ask, first, for a ride back to her place at the harbor.

Only time would tell.

They climbed out of the van and navigated their way over the mound of snow to head toward Diz's big front porch. Clarissa was holding on to Diz's arm as they plowed their way forward, and when they were halfway there, she tugged Diz to a halt.

"That does look awfully forlorn." She pointed at Christa's dark front porch. She looked up at Diz. "Maybe we should have taken Otis up on the wreath?"

Diz nodded and met her eyes.

It was one of those perfect, Hollywood moments, and they both knew it.

The kiss they shared was long and sweet, and full of warmth and promise. It would have gone on a lot longer if a gust of wind rolling down the avenue hadn't loosened a big clump of snow from some place high on Christa's linden tree. It nailed them fair and square. They bolted apart in shock and surprise—then looked up toward the heavens.

"*Jesus H. Christ,*" Clarissa hissed. "Haven't we already had *enough* of this shit for one night?"

Diz raised a hand to try and brush the snow out of her thick hair. "I dunno . . . I think you look kinda *hot* all covered with white icing . . . kinda like my fantasy, dream date."

"You're a pervert." Clarissa was doing her best to try and brush the mound of white powder off her shoulders.

"I do not feel the slightest inclination to disagree." Diz tugged at her arm. "Let's get inside and dry you off."

Clarissa gave her a sultry look. "How did you know I was wet?"

Diz thought she just might dissolve into a warm puddle, herself. Right there on top of the snow.

"Let's go inside," she croaked.

Clarissa laid a restraining hand on her chest. She was looking back up at the linden tree. "Wait a minute . . ."

"What is it?" Diz asked, following her gaze.

Clarissa looked at her. "How many of those obnoxious pink lights did you say were in that big bag?"

"About ten thousand, judging by what I paid for them. Why?"

Clarissa looked up at the snowy branches again.

Diz followed her gaze, then smiled. She suddenly felt even warmer inside.

"I'll go get a ladder," she said.

❉ ❉ ❉

When Diz opened her eyes, the walls of her bedroom were illuminated by a warm, pink glow. In her first, groggy flush of wakefulness, she forgot entirely about the linden tree and assumed the sunrise was portending another rough bout of inclement weather. *What was that old expression? Red sky at morning . . . something, something warning.*

She pushed back the covers and fumbled around to find her robe. Then she made her sleepy way over to the front windows of her room. The pink light coming up from below was seeping in all around the edges of her window blinds. She slowly wound them open so she could look outside.

In fact, it was past dawn. The sky was just beginning to lighten. It was still overcast, but there were hazy slashes of pink-orange visible above the tree line.

Everything outside was blanketed in white. It was like the soft, perfect world inside a snow globe—the one you only got to see once the shaking stopped and the tiny scene inside was allowed to return to its eternally quaint and perfect state of bliss.

In fact, the real world outside her window looked so serene and unspoiled, her breathless admiration of it nearly led her to miss the dark figure standing near the tree.

Christa. Wearing fur-topped boots and an old cloth overcoat of Karl's. She stood there, without moving, bathed in a soft sea of pink light. She was clutching something against her chest. Sunflower seeds. Christa always fed their winter birds in the early morning, before the neighborhood roared to life. Diz watched her as she stood there, staring up at the lighted branches with a hand pressed against her mouth. She dropped her bag of seeds and reached up with both hands to touch the lights that ran along one of the lower branches. In that one moment, Diz could see the years and the sadness melt away from her features. She could imagine that this was precisely how Christa looked when, as a child, her papa would walk her family along the illuminated avenues of Berlin—while she and her brood of brothers waited impatiently for the advent of their beloved Weihnachten.

It was a private moment of hope and joy that she felt gifted to have witnessed. She knew in her heart that she'd never forget it.

She felt something soft brush against the back of her neck. A pair of warm arms wrapped around her from behind.

"Why are you up?" Clarissa asked. "It's still dark."

Diz smiled and leaned back against her. "No it isn't—can't you see the light?"

Clarissa kissed the back of her neck again. Diz felt shivers all the way down to her toes.

"Oh, I've seen the light, all right," she said. "Several times, if you'll recall."

As it happened, Diz could recall. She covered Clarissa's hands with her own. "Christa saw the tree," she said, softly.

Clarissa stifled a laugh. "Diz, I think cosmonauts on the space station could see the tree."

"True." Diz smiled. "We did a good thing. It made her happy."

"I'm glad." Clarissa gave her a warm squeeze. "I'm happy, too."

"You are?"

"Oh, yeah."

Diz got an idea. She turned around to face her. "Wanna unwrap your present?"

Clarissa raised an eyebrow. "You got me a present?"

Diz started to untie the belt on Clarissa's robe. "Oh, yes. Didn't I tell you? It's the best part of the Christmas story. The part where Santa comes *twice*."

Clarissa smiled and backed them both toward the big, warm bed.

❋   ❋   ❋

78

Out front in the center of a snow-covered, urban landscape, a white-haired woman stood rooted in place, smiling up at her stylishly illuminated linden tree. A bag of sunflower seeds lay open on the ground, and several cardinals that had watched her for a time from a distance, finally decided that it was safe enough to approach. They landed near her feet and pecked at the loose seeds that lay strewn across the snow.

It was Christmas morning, and for just a few moments, all was right with the world.

Blended Families

Divide and conquer.

That was the only sane approach.

It was also the only strategy that had a shot at skirting a full-scale nuclear conflagration. And that was especially true if we were seriously thinking about hosting any kind of holiday event that combined Gillespies with Wylies. In my mind, that idea was tantamount to pouring ketchup on a bowl of Cheerios.

Scratch that. The Wylies weren't like a *bowl* of anything—unless it was Almas caviar.

And the Gillespies? Well. The Gillespies were more like a bucket of chicken—heavy on the wings and thighs.

I tapped my red pencil on the notepad. It was no accident that I grabbed one that had next to no eraser left on it. I knew there wasn't going to be anything to cross out because there weren't any scenarios to write down that might have a shot at making this hare-brained scheme work.

"Figure something out," Clarissa said, with her customary head toss. "We have to do this sooner or later. I see no reason to continue putting it off."

Really?

I told her I could see all kinds of reasons to put it off.

"Name one," Clarissa demanded.

I opened my mouth to speak, but she cut me off.

"Not that one."

I glared at her.

"Not that one, either," Clarissa said.

I huffed in frustration. "What do you want from me?"

"Reasons. Not excuses."

"Excuses *are* reasons."

"No they're not."

"Well what the hell are they, then?"

"In your case, excuses are the things you cling to when you're unwilling to confront your fears."

"I thought that was guns and religion?"

"Same difference."

I threw up my hands. "I give up. It's impossible to win an argument with you."

"We finally agree on something." Clarissa checked her watch. She finished her coffee and pushed her chair back. "Look, I have a WebEx meeting at nine. You'll just have to figure this out." She reached across the table and patted the back of my hand. "Put all that copious research you did on deductive reasoning to work. Ask yourself what Poe would do in a similar situation, and do that."

Poe? Poe would've put his head in an oven . . .

I looked up at her. "Honey . . . those are metaphors that even I can't mix."

"Don't underestimate yourself. Remember, I read your entire dissertation."

"Very funny."

"Diz. We're not going to have *two* parties. And neither will we spend our first Christmas as an official couple apart. I already invited my family—more than two weeks ago. They're coming. Christmas Eve is only eight days away. You need to drink a cup of courage and get this done."

"What about Marty and Sheila?" I was pulling out the big guns now.

Clarissa didn't blink. "What about them?"

"They're my family, too." I was pretty sure I sounded like a pouty adolescent. "And Sheila's been really depressed since she lost the baby."

"We've already discussed this. They can come as long as they leave the kids and the Siberian husky locked up in the van." Clarissa got to her feet. "I have to go. Let me know what you figure out."

She kissed me on the head, grabbed her car keys off the counter, and swept out. A sweet, subtle scent of red violets tarried behind her.

That had been nearly two hours ago, and I was no further along.

I was working from home today because I'd been fighting a cold. So far, the cold was winning. The sniffles were making me cranky.

So was trying to figure this mess out. It wasn't that I felt embarrassed by my family. I didn't. It was just that the Gillespies were . . . different. Having my parents over to spend Christmas Eve with the Wileys would be like inviting Ma and Pa Kettle to sit in the Royal Enclosure at Ascot. And this was where I had an advantage over Clarissa. I, at least, knew her father. And believe me, on a bad day Bernard Wiley could make David Niven seem frumpy. He wore handmade suits and Harvard ties. He was a charter member of the Ariel Rowing Club. He drank single malt Scotch that was old enough to vote. I suspected that he would have little in common with Arthur Gillespie, sole proprietor of Art's Back River Crab House in beautiful downtown Essex.

My parents had been running the hole-in-a-wall seafood restaurant for the last decade, ever since my father's retirement from MARC. After twenty-five years of running trains back and forth between Philadelphia's Penn Station and BWI Airport, he decided he was ready to hang up his bandana and pursue his true calling: making really BIG crab cakes.

You have to understand something here. The crab cakes served up at Art's aren't just big, they're ginormous. In fact, being able to eat one of Art's signature Back River Belly Busters adds your photo to a coveted spot on his wall of shame—and earns you an oversized lobster bib that proclaims, "I Ate Art's Big One." Knowing my father, he'd be sure to bring plenty of each along to complement our holiday soirée.

Somehow, I had a hard time imagining Bernard Wiley wearing one of these designer bibs . . . or ever desiring to eat anything larger than his head.

I tried expressing this to Clarissa, but she just waved me off.

"You overdramatize everything," she said.

Not so much. I did have to wonder how it was possible for her to be so unconcerned about mixing crude oil with artesian water. But she was a woman rife with contradictions. Besides, the only member of my family she'd ever met was my brother, Father Frank Gillespie, S.J. That happened about six weeks ago when they both showed up at the police station on Fayette Street to bail Marty and me out of the slammer.

❀ ❀ ❀

It wasn't our fault.

It was a Saturday afternoon, and Marty and I were in his driveway, quietly working on installing a new GPS unit in their minivan. The kids were inside "napping." That meant they were parked in front of the television with Yoo-hoos and an open box of Cheerios. Sheila had announced that she was taking their dog, Sadie, for a walk.

Fifteen minutes later, Marty and I heard the sound of angry voices coming from someplace down the street. Sheila's cheese-grater tones were impossible to mistake. We exchanged forlorn looks over our tangle of tools and wires.

"This can't be good," he said.

We crawled out of the van and headed toward the shouting.

Sheila was embroiled in a fracas with a naked man who was standing outside and screaming at an apparently uncooperative ash tree. True to form, she roared into his yard like Patton invading Sicily and demanded that he put on clothes and quit yelling.

Of course, she didn't seem to care that she was now making more noise than he was.

The naked man told her to shut up and get the hell off his property.

She told him he was a loudmouthed pervert.

He told her she was nosey shrew with a bad haircut.

She told him to fuck off.

He told her to suck his dick.

She told him she'd need a magnifying glass to find it.

He told her she was a lesbian who hated men.

Then it got ugly.

Marty and I arrived on the scene in time to see Sheila haul off and nail the man with a solid right cross. He staggered backward and fell over Sadie, who was already hard at work digging a hole near the base of his holly bush.

Siberian huskies like to dig.

"Oh, jeez . . ." Marty rushed over to help him regain his feet, but the guy smacked his hand away and slugged him. That, of course, made Sheila see even more shades of red. She jumped on top of the naked man and started pummeling him.

"Get this crazy bitch off me," he screamed.

It wasn't happening. Sheila had him pinned in a move that would've won her a title in any Greco Roman wrestling match.

A dazed Marty crawled over and tried to pull Sheila off, but she wasn't budging. Somebody slugged him again. Frankly, the number of arms and legs flying around made it impossible to tell which ones belonged to what person.

I sighed and thought briefly about hiding in the impressive hole Sadie was still digging. I knew this wasn't going to end well.

I gingerly approached the writhing tangle of bodies and did my best to intervene.

"Marty . . . let go of her. Sheila! Stop it . . . *now!* Dude, *please* . . . I'm trying to help out here."

Somebody grabbed hold of my ankle and yanked it out from under me.

Of course, I thought, as I toppled down and landed on top of them all.

Then I heard the sirens.

Six hours later, Marty and I were still cooling our heels in the downtown lockup, waiting for Clarissa to bail us out.

"I still don't see why the cops arrested *us*," Marty complained for the tenth time. Or was it the ten thousandth time?

"Marty," I explained again. "The guy was on his own property. He has the right to yell at any tree he wants."

"Well, what about that buck naked part?"

I shrugged. "He told the police that feeling the breeze on his skin calmed him down."

"And they believed that?"

"Would you rather they arrested Sheila?" I didn't bother to tell him that arresting Sheila would've required a SWAT team and water cannons.

He thought about that. "I guess somebody had to stay with the kids."

I didn't make any reply.

"And now I have to pay for fixing his damn yard, too."

In the space of fifteen minutes, Sadie had done a credible job digging up three holly bushes and a rhododendron. She worked fast.

When we finally got sprung, we were shocked to see my brother standing with Clarissa in the booking area.

Clarissa looked like a thundercloud. Frank just looked . . . amused.

"Who called you?" I asked.

"Sheila." Frank smirked.

Great. Sheila had been a Franciscan nun before she met Marty. She and Frank were thicker than thieves at Calvary.

I gave Clarissa a miserable look. "It wasn't my fault."

She rolled her eyes.

Frank gave her a playful nudge. "I've been filling her in."

"Wonderful," I replied. "Just what I needed."

Clarissa glared at me. "I didn't realize you did your undergraduate work at Leavenworth."

"She's always been an overachiever," Frank quipped.

"You're not helping, Frank." I fixed Clarissa with my best pair of puppy dog eyes.

"Oh, do not even go there." She glowered at me. "It's going to cost you plenty to keep this little tidbit out of the company newsletter."

"I didn't do anything," I complained.

She waved a hand. "You're both just lucky that Mr. Hornhaas is a well-known paraphiliac."

"A what?" Marty asked.

"He likes to wave his junk around in public," Frank explained.

"I got him to drop the charges," Clarissa continued. "But I had to promise that Sheila would attend anger management classes."

I snorted.

Clarissa glared at me. "You're going, too."

"*Me?* What the hell did I do?"

"Let's see." She looked at her watch. "It's nine o'clock on a Saturday night and we're standing here having this conversation in the anteroom of the city jail. Need any other clues?"

I looked down at my shoes. "I guess not."

"Get your stuff and let's get out of here," Frank said. "We're meeting Sheila and the kids at IHOP."

IHOP?

"You're going to IHOP?" I asked Clarissa.

"Of course," she said. "I like pancakes."

I smiled at her. "My little short stack."

She was trying hard not to smile back. "Don't get any ideas. You're still in a lot of trouble."

That wasn't news. I managed to pretty much stay in a lot of trouble.

That's why I was trying hard not to add our first Christmas party to my list of offenses.

I stared at my blank sheet of paper. There was no way to make Clarissa's blended family idea work . . . not without first getting Governor O'Malley to have the National Guard on standby.

The phone rang. I snapped it up.

"Gillespie."

"Yo, Diz." It was Marty.

"What's up?"

"You working from home again today?"

"Yeah. I still feel pretty crappy."

"No better?"

"A little, maybe. Why?"

He sighed. "I need somebody to drop Sadie off at obedience school."

The other part of Clarissa's "deal" with Mr. Hornhaas had been that Sadie needed to learn how to behave. That meant three months of canine juvey.

"Where's Sheila?"

"She's taking the boys to see Santa at the Christmas parade. I was supposed to run by and pick Sadie up, but that asshole Westlake completely rewrote his *Best of Baltimore* column, and I have to have the damn thing edited and ready for production by noon."

"Oh, man . . ."

"Hey . . . I wouldn't ask if it wasn't really important. This damn place dings us for the whole frigging fee if we cancel with less than twenty-four hours notice. It's insane."

I sighed. "Where is it?"

"Charles Village Critters, on St. Paul Street. It's a ten minute walk, max."

I glanced at the wall clock. "What time is she supposed to be there?"

"Eleven-thirty."

"Okay. I'll do it."

"Seriously? Oh, man, you're the best. Really. You know where the spare key is, right? Sadie's harness is on the hook right inside the front door."

"Okay."

"Make sure she heels . . . that's part of her training."

"Right."

"Don't let her yank on the leash. She likes to pull."

"Got it."

"And grab some poop bags . . . she'll probably have to dump two or three times."

"Okay."

"There are some biscuits in a bin inside the closet. You can take some along as treats . . . she minds better when there's a food incentive."

"Roger."

"Be sure you get the *small* ones. She swallows the damn things whole, without chewing. Last time I gave her a big one, she choked and we had to give her the Heimlich maneuver."

"Marty . . ."

"She shot that thing all the way across the hall into the family room."

"Marty . . ."

"It nearly took out Alvin's eye."

"Marty . . ."

"Sheila put one of those Boca burgers on it to keep the swelling down."

"Marty . . ."

"Teddy was pretty pissed . . . he wasn't finished eating it yet."

"Marty!"

"What?"

"Jeez Louise. I got it, okay?"

"You didn't have to yell."

I sighed. "If I don't get going, I won't get her there in time."

"Hold on a second." I could hear someone else in the background muttering. He came back on the line. "Hey, I gotta run. You'll have to finish your story later."

He hung up.

I shook my head and put the phone down.

The last thing I felt like doing was taking Marty's psycho dog for a walk. The only bright spot was that the obedience school was in the same general area as the Baltimore Bicycle Works. And I wanted to stop in and take a look at Clarissa's Christmas present—a brand new Bianchi Metropoli Uno. I ordered it three weeks ago, and they called me yesterday to let me know that it had arrived. The sleek hybrid was perfect for Clarissa, who'd never had a bike growing up. It was solid and stylish and well suited for navigating the curbs and potholes of city streets. Plus it was Italian. And Clarissa loved anything Italian.

I hoped she'd like it. I looked forward to many happy outings with her.

Thinking about giving it to her made me smile.

And that made me think about what a putz I was being about the party. Inviting both of our families to a holiday celebration was a big step for Clarissa. It was a bold and public acknowledgement of our relationship. And it was a precursor to her moving in. She wanted everyone to see us together in a home environment before unveiling those plans. It was wrong for me to let my uneasiness spoil her best intentions. If she could afford to be so magnanimous, then so could I.

I glanced at the wall clock again. I still had about ten minutes before I needed to leave for Marty's. I pulled my laptop over and quickly typed up the details of our party. I filled in the email addresses of my parents, my brother, and Marty and Sheila. My finger hovered for a moment over the mouse. I had a momentary sense of impending catastrophe . . . like the one Mrs. O'Leary's cow probably felt as soon as that lantern went over.

I took a deep breath.

Clarissa was right. It was ridiculous to be so superstitious.

I closed my eyes and clicked "send."

❁ ❁ ❁

Sadie didn't just yank on her leash; she damn near pulled my arm out of its socket. I fought her for the first six blocks, then just gave up and started trotting along behind her. It seemed to work better that way.

It didn't help that it was cold as hell. The temperature had plummeted overnight and, even though the sun was out, it was still well below freezing. The frigid air was burning my lungs. I tried to rein Sadie in so I could stop and catch my breath. At this rate, I'd end up with bronchitis before we reached St. Paul Street.

Christmas was only a week away, and most of the shops were advertising blowout sales. All the city decorations were starting to look a bit frazzled. The big weather systems that kept rolling up from the south were bringing more rain than snow, and everything just looked . . . gray.

A sidewalk vendor up ahead was selling hot sausages. Sadie seemed entirely too interested by that prospect, so I decided to cross the street. Some of the houses along this block had what could only be called eclectic decorations. Most of them looked like mini shrines to the Baltimore Ravens. Santas wearing bright purple jerseys, tinsel wrapped goal posts, and trees festooned with tiny footballs dotted the front lawns of several homes. It was festive and tacky, in a consistent and decidedly Baltimore way.

Even Sadie stopped to admire the spectacle. But that was short-lived. A squirrel fell out of a tree and had the great misfortune to land within three feet of her nose. The only thing that saved it was the scrap of iron fence that separated us from it. Sadie lunged toward the fence like she'd been shot from a cannon, dragging me along behind her. I'm surprised that her momentum wasn't enough to slam us both between the rusty bars.

The squirrel took off and ran north along the fence line with Sadie in hot pursuit. I still had hold of her leash and I was doing my best to try and slow her down. We were nearly at the intersection of East 22nd Street. The squirrel switched back and roared up the side of an Ash tree before jumping over to the eaves spout on a house. Sadie stopped on a dime but my forward momentum kept me going. I tumbled over her and landed face down in a half frozen puddle of muddy slush. I cursed and rolled up into a sitting position and glowered at Sadie, who was paying no attention to me at all. She sat stiffly at attention, staring with criminal intent at the chattering squirrel, which was flipping us off from its perch on an outcropping of gutter.

I shook my gloved hands and tried to wipe the worst of muck off the front of my jacket. It cut a ludicrous, brackish-colored swath from my shoulders to my thighs.

"Thanks a bunch, dog."

Sadie's steel blue eyes never so much as blinked in my direction, but I noticed her left ear twitch. At least I counted that as some kind of recognition.

I sighed and looked up the street. At least we were only a block from the damn doggie reform school. I still had five minutes to get her there on time. Maybe they'd take pity on me and let me try and clean up in their restroom.

I climbed to my feet and gave a sharp yank on Sadie's leash.

"Come on, Scarface. You've got a date with destiny."

My gloves were soaked, and I could feel my fingers starting to freeze. I was also pretty sure that my knees were skinned-up beneath my jeans. Sadie, of course, was now trotting along beside me in a perfect imitation of a well-heeled dog.

I wanted to clobber her.

I noticed that I was getting odd looks from passers-by. It wasn't hard to imagine why. I'm certain it was abundantly clear to the holiday masses that a mud-covered vagrant with a sour expression was stealing this perfectly behaved, immaculately groomed Siberian husky. No doubt they all would see my picture on the evening news. Of course, everyone would think it was the famous news anchor being implicated in a holiday dognapping scheme instead of me.

And that would mean more record-breaking audience shares in the Baltimore market for my look-alike, Rachel Maddow.

That woman really owed me big time.

We nearly reached the entrance to Charles Village Critters. A shiny black Mercedes pulled over to the curb and stopped. A waifish-looking woman dressed to the nines in gray cashmere and Jackie-O sunglasses climbed out. She was holding some kind of designer-type dog that looked like a four-footed replica of her: expensive and incredibly high

93

maintenance. They were even dressed alike. The dog wore a dove gray coat with a fur-lined collar. I wasn't certain about its breed. A Whippet, maybe? It was something nervous and whiny.

The white-haired woman gingerly sat the dog down on the ground and turned to address the driver of the Mercedes.

Then it happened.

Sadie and the dog saw each other.

It was like the heavens parted. I swore I could hear the finale from *Kismet* rolling out along the boulevard. Ruth Anne Swenson and Samuel Ramey going full-tilt boogie in an all-star duet of "Stranger in Paradise."

Sadie jerked to a halt. She and the Whippet stared at each other across the expanse of chipped concrete, parking meters, and potted plants. Time stood still.

It was love . . . or something very much akin to it.

Sadie emitted an ear-splitting chirp. It was one of those high-pitched, fingernails on a chalkboard sounds that Siberian husky's make in lieu of barks.

The Whippet answered her with a shriek that rolled out like a tsunami warning.

Sadie's call sounded again. Soon a medley of whines rose up and twisted together in the cold air. It was every bit as atonal as a chorus of cheap coffee grinders.

Then the unthinkable happened.

Just as the Mercedes pulled away, the Whippet broke free and flounced toward us on a wave of gray cashmere.

The wispy woman who had been holding onto its leash stumbled and nearly fell as she attempted to lunge for the escaping dog.

"Maris! Stop!" she bellowed.

Maris?

I did my best to plant my feet and cinch up Sadie's leash, but I knew it was going to be a lost cause. Even a twenty-mule team pulling a load of borax across Death Valley would be unable to stop Sadie if she wanted to run. And right now, Sadie wanted to run.

I gave it my best effort. I held on long enough to walk away with top honors at any bronco busting championship. The leash I had wrapped around my hand was pulled so tight I could feel my fingers starting to tingle. My feet were sliding across the sidewalk as Sadie dragged me along behind her.

The wispy woman was lurching toward us. She had a curious, bobbing gait—like someone trying to jump hurdles with a stiff leg. Then I realized that she'd broken the heel on one of her ridiculously high shoes.

Maris reached Sadie. The two dogs balanced on their hind legs and danced around each other in a nearly perfect imitation of an Arthur Murray routine.

And cha-cha-cha, break and swivel . . .

They were still caterwauling.

"Get that *thing* off my Maris!" the wispy woman croaked. She sounded like a smoker.

I didn't bother to point out that her Maris was actually the one on top of the *thing*.

"I'm doing my best, lady." I circled the two dogs, looking for the best opening to reach in and grab Sadie by the harness.

Sadie had two-thirds of Maris's head inside her mouth.

"Oh my *god!* That thing is eating my baby." The woman was nearly hysterical. She kicked at Sadie with her broken shoe. "Stop. Stop it."

"Stop kicking her," I yelled. "They're *playing*—they're not hurting each other."

"Your dog is killing my Maris!" she screamed.

Passing cars slowed down. Pedestrians stopped to watch the spectacle.

The woman flailed at the dogs. I let go of Sadie's leash and stepped over to haul her back.

"Stop it." I held her firmly by the shoulders and gave her a little shake. "They're just *playing*. Dogs *do* that. You need to calm down."

"How dare you." The small woman was surprisingly strong. "Get your hands off me. You and that thing of yours should be locked up."

She kicked me with her one good shoe. Hard.

"Jeez, lady." I jumped back, expecting to see a four-inch heel projecting from the top of my foot. "What the hell is the matter with you?"

But she wasn't paying any attention to me. She was pointing, open mouthed, at the empty sidewalk behind us.

The dogs were gone.

"Where is she?" She gave me a murderous look. "If anything happens to my Maris, there won't be enough of you left to bury."

I looked about frantically.

A burly man in a buffalo plaid jacket was leaning against a parking meter, smoking. He raised a meaty hand and pointed up St. Paul Street with his cigarette.

"They went that away," he said.

I scanned the area in time to see the flash of Sadie's white behind as she rounded the corner on 25th Street—plainly in hot pursuit of Maris.

Perfect.

One of the fastest dogs on the planet was now being chased by one of the most stubborn.

The angry, wispy woman was wailing and screaming for the police.

I considered my options.

If any of us survived, I'd get to spend a lifetime making Marty pay . . .

I took off after the dogs.

❈ ❈ ❈

"Gillespie!"

The big iron door rolled back. I looked up from my seat on the low bunk. Late afternoon light was filtering in through a high, transom window at the end of the corridor. Something about this place was starting to feel downright homey. It exuded a calm that was mostly missing in the rest of my life. I knew that I'd be sorry to leave it—especially when I had to confront what I knew would be waiting for me outside in central processing.

I'd used my one phone call to reach out to my brother, Father Frank. Again.

I asked him to wear his collar this time.

This time. Jeez . . .

At the rate I was going, I should ask the City of Baltimore for a time-share on this joint.

But it did occur to me that maybe having a big, jovial priest bail me out would lend a holiday flavor to my misfortune. Why not add a little *Bells of St. Mary's* flourish to lessen the sting of my most recent crime against humanity—especially since I knew that both of the dogs were safe and sound?

Which, by the way, was more than I could say for my unhappy prospects.

I couldn't begin to imagine how I was going to explain this one to Clarissa. Somehow the words, "It wasn't my fault," rang hollow—even to me. And not just because I'd said them the last time I ended up here.

I followed along behind the matron as we headed for the discharge area.

"See ya on the flip side, Dorrie." I waved at the big woman in the first cell who apparently was a fixture in this particular lockup.

"Later, doll face." Dorrie gave me a two-fingered salute.

It took a minute for my eyes to adjust to the fluorescent light in the discharge area. I didn't see Frank. Just my luck he'd pick today to run a few errands on his way downtown to bail his baby sister out of the joint.

There were six or eight other people seated around the room on beat up wooden benches. Most of them looked tired and bored, and entirely used to being precisely where they were.

Then I saw her. My heart skipped a beat.

Uh oh . . .

Clarissa.

She did not look happy.

I opened my mouth to ask what she was doing there, but she raised a hand to stop me.

"Don't. Say. Anything."

I sighed and walked to the window to claim my belongings.

Clarissa was silent on the entire ride back to my house. I was dying to ask how she found out about what had happened, but I was afraid to do so. I knew she'd tell me when she was good and ready.

"Can you at least tell me where the dogs are?" I asked, timidly.

She glared at me. "Home where they belong.

I didn't speak again and neither did she.

When we got home and entered the house, Clarissa tossed her coat and bag down on a chair and headed straight for the liquor cabinet.

That wasn't good news. Clarissa rarely drank the hard stuff, and I'd never known her to indulge on weekdays—or during broad daylight.

She held up a bottle of Remy. "Want some?"

That was something, at least. I nodded vigorously and headed for the kitchen to retrieve two glasses.

When I got back to the living room, she had collapsed on the sofa and flipped on the gas logs. I set the two tumblers down on the coffee table in front of her and turned on the lights on the Christmas tree.

"Feeling festive?" she asked. Her words were like jabs from an ice pick.

I shrugged.

Our tree this year was more modest in scale than the trees I'd had in years past. This one was a solid six-footer. A Frasier Fir from Ash County, North Carolina. In addition to the strands of blazing blue-and-white lights, the tree was covered with tiny red-and-black paper birds. Cardinals and Ravens . . . my eternal emblems of hope and despair.

Today the fifty-fifty odds they presented seemed more appropriate than ever.

Clarissa poured us each a hefty dose of the cognac. I sat down on the sofa at a safe distance from her and picked up my glass.

"Are you ever going to ask me about what happened?"

"I already *know* what happened." Her voice was still icy.

"Well maybe you'd like to fill me in, then—since I kinda lost track after the parade?"

She sighed and sipped her cognac. Then she shifted her position and faced me.

"I changed my mind."

I was confused. "About what?"

"I want to hear your version of events."

My version?

"What other version is there?" I asked.

She waved a hand dismissively. "Don't prevaricate."

I sighed. "The dogs took off and I chased after them. When I finally caught up to them at the Christmas parade, I got arrested. End of story."

"End of story?"

I nodded.

"I think your CliffsNotes summary omits a few pertinent details."

"Such as?" I was starting to squirm.

"Let's see." She tipped her head back while she tallied up the missing details. "Aggravated assault. Disorderly conduct. Personal and public property damages totaling more than $42,856, disruption of the Mayor's Christmas Parade, and indecent exposure."

"Indecent exposure?" I asked, incredulous.

Clarissa raised an eyebrow.

"Oh . . ." I remembered. "That."

"Yes. *That.*"

"Come on. That one was *so* not my fault."

"And the other litany of crimes?"

"Well . . ."

Clarissa sighed. "Diz? You do realize that you're going to be the centerfold in tonight's police report?"

I hung my head. "I was trying to catch them."

"Well, you certainly succeeded."

"Hey. It's not my fault that blue-haired pit viper called the cops."

"She wasn't the only one."

I thought about it. "I guess those people at the Baltimore Museum of Art were pretty pissed, huh?"

"You might say that. I don't think they appreciated having two marauding dogs roar through the star-studded opening reception for the Marguerite Matisse exhibit."

I ran a hand over my face. "Their leashes got tangled up around the legs of the buffet table. Those canapés went everyplace."

"I know."

"I honestly don't know how Sadie managed to eat four platters of them before the security guards chased them back toward the front door."

"Diz . . ."

"She puked three times in the foyer."

"Diz . . ."

"Of course, that damn Whippet ate her puke."

"Diz . . ."

"Then she threw up, too."

Clarissa closed her eyes.

"I actually think that crabmeat was bad . . . she probably did them all a favor."

Clarissa dropped a hand to my arm and squeezed. Her grip was like a vice.

I winced. "What?"

"Stop. Just. Stop."

"You asked me to tell you what happened." I sulked.

Clarissa shook her head.

"I don't think those Cone sisters would've complained," I grumbled. "They liked dogs . . . and art."

"Oh, really? Too bad you can't say the same thing about the administration at Johns Hopkins."

I rolled my eyes. "They were asking for it."

"Excuse me?" Clarissa was giving me her vintage "you're insane" look.

I waved a hand. "What in the hell were they thinking, holding a damn Winter Wonderland festival with live animals from the Baltimore Zoo?"

"Diz. It took them nearly three hours to round up all those penguins."

"How is that *my* fault? Those damn birds were all over the place, flapping around like lunatics, chasing that freak-show Whippet. The damn thing was trailing a five-foot string of red hots it picked up after knocking over that sidewalk vendor in Wyman Park."

Clarissa drained her glass and picked up the bottle. "I can't listen to any more of this."

"Hey . . . you asked to hear *my* version of events. Well. This is my version of events."

She sighed and refilled her glass. "Tell me about the parade."

The parade.

She meant the annual Mayor's Christmas Parade. The one Sheila and the kids were attending—which was the whole reason I was stuck with Sadie in the first place.

The two rampaging hounds from hell finally chose this as the signature event to end their metropolitan reign of terror.

Demoralized, exhausted, and nearly dead from running flat out in the frigid air, I finally caught up with the dogs at the intersection of 36th Street and Chestnut Avenue. I could hear the distant rumble of marching bands as the parade approached. My lungs were burning, and I was gasping for air. I thought I might pass out. Then I saw them.

Sadie and Maris were cooling their heels near a roadside water station when I limped up behind them. I nearly had a hand on Sadie before she whipped her head around at the last instant and saw me just as I made a grab for her harness. I feinted to the right in a lame attempt to trick her, but she was too quick. And smart. She knew it was a ruse and plunged right on past me, with the cashmere-clad Maris in tow.

"I nearly had them there," I explained to Clarissa. I held up my thumb and index finger. "It was *this* close. But that damn husky outsmarted me."

"There's a shocker," Clarissa said without a trace of empathy."

"Hey!" I socked her on the leg. "I'd like to see you go twelve rounds with a Siberian husky on crack and still be standing up to talk about it."

Clarissa sipped from her glass. "What happened next?"

"Next?" I shook my head. "Next I collapsed against a light pole and watched the parade roll by. It wasn't until I heard the roar and applause from the crowd that I looked up and saw the two dogs riding on the back of Santa's float."

She glared at me. "And then you got arrested."

"Not exactly. It took a while for the crowds to realize what the dogs were actually *doing* up there."

Clarissa narrowed her eyes.

"It wasn't until the float passed the reviewing stand that the commotion started. Of course, this is the precise moment when that she-bitch Skeletor arrived on the scene. She started shrieking her over-permed head off when she saw her precious Maris splayed out atop a supine, spread-eagled Siberian husky, licking away like there was no tomorrow."

Clarissa covered her face with her free hand.

"People were yelling and yanking their kids away. The Santa on the front of the float was totally oblivious. He just kept waving and yelling, 'Ho, ho, ho . . . Merry Christmas.' It didn't help that the corporate sponsor of the float was Urbanspoon's *Taste of Baltimore*."

Clarissa's shoulders were shaking now.

"Then Skeletor grabbed a nearby policeman and told him I was a pervert who had stolen her prize show dog. I had just started to explain the situation to him when I heard the approaching sound of Sheila's ear-splitting voice screaming at me for losing her dog. The last thing I heard before I got shoved into the backseat of a patrol car was Alvin asking Sheila what that dog in the gray coat was doing on top of Sadie."

Clarissa was doing a bad job trying not to laugh. She wouldn't make eye contact with me.

"They told me that Sheila got Sadie back, and I assume that Skeletor got her precious Whippet. I honestly have no idea why I'm the one who ended up in the joint. Again." I looked at her. "I called Father Frank to come down and bail me out. I assume he's the one who ratted me out and told you I was there?"

Clarissa didn't reply right away.

"Well?" I asked.

She shrugged. "Not exactly. It turns out you weren't the only one arrested at the parade."

I wasn't? This was news.

"Who else got picked up?"

She sighed. "The owner of the Whippet got taken in, too. Apparently, she slapped someone in the crowd for making a lewd comment about her dog's . . . proclivities."

"Ha!" I laughed. "Serves her right. What a crusty old bitch. She deserves to have a lesbo dog."

"And daughter, apparently."

"What are you talking about?"

"Diz. That crusty old bitch was Elspeth Wiley."

"*Elspeth?*" I waved a hand. "Of *course* she'd have a name like Elspeth. Who in the hell has a name like Elspeth?" I shook my head. Clearly someone who names her dog Maris.

Wait a minute . . .

Wiley?

I looked at Clarissa with a sinking feeling. "Did you say her name was Elspeth Wiley?"

"That's right." She nodded. "Although I generally just call her Mom."

❊ ❊ ❊

"You have to come out eventually."

"No, I don't."

I heard her rattle the doorknob.

"Diz. Unlock the door."

"No."

"Honey. You can't spend the night in the powder room. It's not that bad."

"That's easy for you to say. You're not the one whose face is plastered all over the six o'clock news."

"Neither are you. Everyone thinks it was Rachel Maddow who got arrested."

Cold comfort.

"Did you hear what they're calling it?" I whined. "*The Great Santa Paws Caper.* That's what they said on WJZ."

"I heard it."

"What kind of lame ass headline was that?"

"You're upset about the headline?"

"Aren't you? I give them the story of the century and *The Great Santa Paws Caper* is the best they can come up with? Someone should revoke their FCC license."

"Honey . . ."

"I can't do anything right, Clar. I really fucked things up."

"No you didn't."

"Oh, yeah?" I huffed. "Try telling that to *Elspeth.*"

103

"Diz . . ."

"She's going to sue me for those damages."

"Diz . . ."

"It'll take me the rest of my natural life to raise that much money."

"Honey . . ."

"And she'll never let you see me again when she finds out about us."

"Diz, don't be ridiculous. I'm not Rapunzel. What do you think they'll do? Cut off my hair?"

"No . . . your allowance."

There was silence on the other side of the door.

I felt like a schmuck.

"I'm sorry."

No response.

"Clar?"

All quiet on the western front.

I unlocked the door and stepped out of the powder room. Clarissa was sitting on the floor with her back against the wall and her legs stretched out across the sisal rug. She was holding the Remy bottle. I did not see a glass. I could, however, see the reflection of the Christmas tree lights in her gray eyes as she looked up at me.

"I'm an asshole," I said.

"I'm not inclined to disagree with you."

I slid down the wall to sit beside her. "Why do you put up with me?"

She looked at me. For once, her expression was unguarded. "Because I think you're adorable."

I felt that tingling again. The same one I'd experienced earlier in the day when my fingers were starting to freeze. It started in all my extremities and quickly spread out along my arms and legs to jump-start all my bigger parts. Clarissa was like a human piezo igniter.

"I am?"

She nodded. "You're also funny, uncommonly smart, sweetly dorky, and a loyal friend. Plus you look exactly like Rachel Maddow." She smiled. "What's not to love?"

I wanted to crawl inside her and wrap her words around me like a thermal blanket. "You love me?"

She rolled her eyes. "Yes, Diz. I love you. And not in spite of my better judgment, but because of it."

I smiled stupidly and leaned into her.

"However, there is one thing we need to get straight."

Shit. I knew it was too good to be true.

"I have my own resources which are not—I repeat, *not*—dependent upon support or patronage from my parents, or anyone else. Are we clear on that?"

I nodded.

"I mean it. I don't want to have this discussion again."

I crossed my heart with two fingers. "I promise."

"Good." She passed me the Remy bottle. "Drink up. There's more."

"Oh, man." I took the bottle and drank a hefty sip. It went down like polished fire.

"I talked with Dad."

"Oh shit." I slumped against her.

"I told him about us. I mean, I told him the parts he hadn't already figured out."

I was stunned. "You told him?"

"Under the circumstances, it seemed indicated."

I looked down at the floor. "I guess so."

She bumped my shoulder. "Don't be so glum. Dad likes you. He always has."

"He might like me as an employee of Wiley Magazine Group. I'm not so sure how he'll feel about me as your . . . you know."

"My . . . you know?"

I shrugged. "Yeah."

"I'm not even sure how *I'd* feel about you as my 'you know.'"

She smirked. "You know?"

"Very funny."

"Lighten up, honey. It wasn't exactly rocket science for him to connect the dots. Not after my desperation to get to you during that blizzard last year on Christmas Eve."

"He figured that one out, huh?"

"You might say that. My zeal to hitch a ride with the redoubtable Beaver Cab Company during the snowstorm of the decade probably tipped my cards just a tad. My father has always been a quick study."

I smiled at the recollection of how Clarissa showed up at Otis Campbell's tree lot like a creature from the storm. Fond memories of how the rest of that night panned out made me smile even more. She noticed.

"What are you thinking about?"

"One guess."

"Pervert."

"Hey? Unlike you, I've never pretended to be otherwise."

She rolled her eyes and held out her hand. "Give me that."

I passed the Remy bottle over. She took a sip.

"Are we gonna sit here all night?" I asked.

"I dunno." She shrugged. "At least until the cognac runs out."

I sighed.

"What is it?" she asked.

"I was thinking about Elspeth."

"Oh. Yeah. I fear that one is going to be a harder sell."

"You think?"

"Dad says we should wait until the party and let her be surprised."

I looked at her with alarm. "Is he nuts?"

"Not usually. But Mom is totally preoccupied right now with Maris's therapy, and he doesn't want to overtax her."

"Excuse me?" I wasn't sure I'd heard her correctly. "Did you say *therapy*?"

She nodded.

"For the *dog*?"

She nodded again.

"Maris has a therapist?"

"So it seems."

I was dumbfounded. "How is that even possible?"

She handed me the cognac bottle.

"Let's see. You take one part over-bred dog, two parts over-bred dog owner, and three parts disposable income. Shake all together and voila—Jungian veterinarian with offices overlooking the Inner Harbor."

"Do the Obamacare people know about this?"

"I don't think it's covered."

106

I shook my head. "And I'm worried about how I'm going to come up with $42,000 in damages."

Clarissa smiled. "By the way . . . I've been meaning to ask you about that."

"About what?"

"The damages. In actual fact, the dog owners are the ones responsible for the debt."

"So?"

"So that would be my mother and Marty. Not you. Yet you keep talking about this like it's your responsibility."

"It is."

"How so?"

"Well." I pulled my legs up and rubbed my hands over my sore knees. "Sadie was in my care when she got loose." I looked up at Clarissa. "And there's no way Marty and Sheila could ever take on a debt like that—not with three kids."

I thought I could see her eyes soften as she looked back at me. "Even if I agreed with you—and I'm not saying that I do—there are probably some opportunities to reduce this amount."

I looked at her with interest. "Such as?"

"My father happens to be on the Museum board, and he's also a trustee at Hopkins."

I perked up at once. "Did you say he liked me?"

"Not as much as he likes my mother—and values his reputation."

I smiled. "Good ol' Bernie."

Clarissa held up a hand. "Hold your applause. He has a condition."

My heart sank. "What is it?"

"You have to promise to refrain from committing any felonies in the State of Maryland for at least six months."

"Doesn't anyone care that I was framed? On *both* occasions?"

"You're forgetting that my mother was arrested, too."

I looked at her. "I'm certain that her record has already been expunged."

"More than likely."

I sighed. "I'll miss seeing Dorrie. I was thinking about inviting her to our party."

"Dorrie?"

"My cell mate in the joint. She's really been misunderstood, too."

Clarissa rolled her eyes. "Let's not and say we did."

We sat in silence for a few moments. I could hear Perry Como crooning from the front room. I didn't realize that Clarissa had turned on the stereo.

"I met a man who lived in Tennessee. He was heading for . . ."

I thought about the party again. "I did it, you know."

Clarissa looked at me with alarm. "Did what?"

"Invited my family. I did it. I sent them all invitations."

She seemed surprised. "You did?"

I nodded. "Marty and Sheila, too."

She smiled. It was one of her high-octane smiles. The ones that made my insides melt. She leaned into me. Red violets.

"That wasn't so hard, was it?" Her voice was low and soft.

"I guess we'll see. I hope your father likes crab cakes."

She rested her hand on top of mine. "He loves crab cakes."

"Really big ones?" I asked.

"Uh huh." Her face was very close to mine now. It filled up my plane of vision. But I could still see the reflection of the tree lights in her gleaming eyes.

"I'm talking the kind that could declare statehood."

"So I've heard." She gently took the Remy bottle away from me and set it out of harm's way.

"You have to see them to believe them."

"Diz?"

"What?"

"Shut up."

She kissed me, and I had a fleeting, euphoric sense that maybe this whole blended-family scheme of hers might actually work. But as our nonverbal conversation progressed, I stopped thinking about crab cakes, relatives, dogs, and dog therapists and concentrated instead on the one sweet combination that always worked just like a charm.

❉   ❉   ❉

"Oh, there is no fucking way!"

I grabbed the remote control and punched in the numbers for another channel. The screen filled up with another big map of the eastern United States. All of the Mid-Atlantic States were colored with a big swath of blue. Dark blue.

The talking heads were rhapsodizing about something called "Winter Storm Brunhilde," the fast-moving, surprise low pressure system that had materialized in the gulf and was now roaring up the coast dumping ice and snow in its wake. Local forecasters seemed to have divided opinions on exactly what track Brunhilde would take when she reached the Chesapeake. Most of the computer models suggested that Brunhilde would head out to sea well before she reached the Baltimore-Washington metropolitan area. A minority of other models suggested that we needed to prepare for yet another white Christmas.

I had my money on the minority opinions. The way my luck was running, we'd probably be looking at whiteout conditions within the next twenty minutes.

Of course, that might mean we'd have to cancel the party . . .

I smiled.

Last year's Christmas Eve blizzard worked out really well for me. Clarissa and I finally ended up together—and we'd been together ever since.

There were worse outcomes than having to spend an entire evening dodging daggers thrown my way by a creature named Elspeth, and inventing ways to prevent my father from challenging Bernard Wiley to eat one of his big ones.

I couldn't even think about the permutations of horror that awaited us by adding Marty and Sheila to the mix.

Nope. This surprise storm was going to be a godsend. No two ways about it.

Clarissa came out of the bathroom and picked up her suit jacket.

I pointed at the mostly-blue weather map that dominated the TV screen.

"Honey—" I began.

She cut me off.

"Forget about it. We're not canceling."

"But the weather people are saying—"

"The weather people are saying that it's going to fizzle before it reaches us. We're supposed to be in the mid-forties by six o'clock tonight."

"Clar . . ."

"Forget about it, Diz. We're *not* canceling. The catering is ordered. The invitations are sent. The decorations are up. Your goose is cooked." She pulled on her watch and snapped it into place. "Find a way to make peace with it. This party is happening."

I tossed the remote onto the bed in frustration.

"What good are two-hundred-and-forty high-def cable channels when you don't listen to any of them?"

She stopped in the center of the room and glared at me.

"I don't need two-hundred-and-forty high-def cable channels to get the weather. I have an iPhone." She buttoned her jacket. "And by the way, half of those two-hundred-and-forty high-def channels are part of that deluxe cartoon package you *had* to have."

"I love Bullwinkle." I sulked.

"I know you do, sweetheart." She walked to me and kissed my forehead. "Learn to love this party, too. It'll make both of our lives a lot easier."

"Okay." I gave her a crooked smile. "Will you be nice to me if I do?"

She narrowed her eyes. "Define *nice*."

I ran a hand over her firm, wool-clad bottom. "I'd rather show you."

She rolled her eyes and swatted my hand away. "In your dreams."

"Exactly." I pulled her close for a kiss.

She tolerated it for most of a minute.

Well . . . maybe for a minute and a half.

Then she pulled away. "I have to get to work, and so do you."

"I don't wanna go to work." I nuzzled her soft neck. "You smell good."

"Bathing does have its advantages." She patted the back of my head. "Will you be home by four?"

I nodded. Our guests would begin arriving at six-thirty.

"Good. I'll do my best to be here before five." She gave me another quick kiss. "Try not to worry so much. It will all work out just fine."

"I hope so."

She smiled at me and headed for the stairs. I stood in the center of the room and listened as she crossed the living room, collected her keys from the top of the bookcase, and went out the kitchen door.

I glanced again at the big, flat screen. The Weather Channel was now airing fantastic video of an ice storm paralyzing Charlotte, ruining Christmas Eve celebrations for thousands.

"Yeah." I snapped up the remote control and shut off the TV. "In my dreams, all right."

❄ ❄ ❄

I did make it home by four o'clock, but not because of the party.

Sleet started falling in Baltimore a little after nine a.m. During the late morning, ominous streaks of heavy snow broke out south of the city. The big bands of white stuff surged northward as a second low-pressure system quickly intensified. By noon, heavy snow had settled in over much of the area, and forecasters were all scratching their heads. The snow continued falling at rates of up to three inches per hour for several hours, accompanied by lightning and thunder. Temperatures were hovering around the thirty-degree mark, and since the texture of the snow was heavy and wet, power outages were predicted to become a problem by nightfall.

Accumulation predictions ranged anywhere from six-to-sixteen inches, with a foot being most favored.

Traffic tie-ups were already dominating news headlines. Fifteen and twenty-two mile backups were reported on Interstates 95 and 70 in and around Baltimore. Already, an estimated sixty-thousand commuters were reportedly stuck in traffic.

It was shaping up to be a shitty night for a party.

I quickly realized that if I didn't head out for home soon, I'd end up spending the night on the floor in our Xerox room. And unlike previous years, I had no interest in amusing myself with the attentions

111

of Randi and Ronni, the twins who ran our company's duplicating center.

I called Clarissa's office before I hitched a ride home with Marty. She picked up on the first ring.

"We're not canceling," she said, before I had a chance to identify myself.

"Hello to you, too," I replied.

"I knew it was you."

"Then you also know that down here in the bowels of the building, we have no windows."

"Your point would be?"

"Have you looked outside recently?"

"Of course."

I sighed. "And?"

"And . . . it's snowing."

"It's not just snowing . . . it's snowing a lot."

"Diz. We're not canceling."

"What is it with you and this damn party? Nobody in their right mind is going to want to be out in this mess tonight."

"All the people who matter to us will be there."

It was clear that arguing with her was useless. For some reason, this damn party had become her hill to die on.

"Do you want to hitch a ride home with Marty and me?"

"When are you leaving?"

"As soon as I hang up."

I could tell she was thinking it over.

"Does he still have that Simply Red CD stuck in the stereo?"

"Of course."

"I think I'll pass."

"Honey—"

"Besides, I have one more thing I have to take care of today."

"Can't it wait?"

"No."

"Clar . . ."

"Diz, I promise to be home within the hour."

I didn't say anything.

"I promise," she said again. "Okay?"

"Okay." I sighed. "I'm going to get going now."

"See you at home. Be careful riding in that thing."

"You be careful, too. That car of yours isn't made for weather like this."

"It'll do fine." I could hear voices and laughter in the background. "I have to run now, sweetie. My three-thirty is here. I'll see you in a bit."

I opened my mouth to say "I love you," but she'd already disconnected.

Such was life upstairs in the posh editorial suite.

I looked around my basement office. Tossing a few coats of brightly colored paint on all the conduit and plumbing pipes didn't make this place any homier. It still looked like the set of Fritz Lang's *Metropolis*. Down here in the dank catacombs, the lower echelon of Wiley employees plodded through their days without notice. I still didn't understand why research departments always got crammed into the darkest parts of buildings. Did people think we were troglophiles?

I shut down the computer and stared at my reflection in the monitor.

I did sort of look like a cave dweller . . .

Maybe I needed to change my glasses.

Then Marty was at the door snapping his fingers, and we were on our way.

It only took us twenty-five minutes to get to our neighborhood—not too bad, considering the traffic jams on all the major thoroughfares. Marty navigated the back alleys and byways of the city like a Romanian cab driver. I'd lived in Baltimore most of my life, and I'd never seen some of the streets he zigzagged across as we threaded our way home.

"I didn't know we still had a Chicken Delight."

He nodded. "Their ribs are the best."

I sunk lower in my seat. "I don't think they'll be doing very much business tonight."

Five minutes later, he turned onto my street. I noticed two things right away.

My next door neighbor, Christa, had strung the hot pink, LED lights I bought her last year—but this time, they were looped around her porch railings and not on the linden tree in her front yard. They made a dazzling spectacle against the falling snow.

The other discovery was my father's massive Buick, which was completely blocking our driveway.

It begins.

"Is that your dad's car?" Marty asked.

The rear bumper was covered with stickers that read, "Eat Art's Big One."

"How'd you guess?"

He chuckled. "It looks like I'm leaving you in good hands."

I touched him on the arm. "You won't ditch out on me tonight, will you?"

"And miss seeing this eclectic off-Broadway production of *Meet the Parents?* Do I look nuts?"

"Okay." I opened my door. "Just remember what I said about that felonious dog and its three henchmen."

He nodded. "They're locked in the attic. Got it."

I climbed out and trudged my way up the rapidly disappearing sidewalk to the house.

My mother met me at the door. Her ensemble was brighter than the Christmas tree aisle at Walmart. She looked like an ageing refugee from an *Annie Hall* remake.

"What the hell are you wearing?" I asked. I stomped my feet and did my best to shake the snow off my jacket.

She did a little pirouette in the foyer. "Like it? I just found this fantastic little import shop—all organic fabrics. These batik prints are all made with sustainable dyes."

"It looks like a UNICEF card."

"That's what I thought." She slapped me on the arm. "Get in here. Your father is cooking."

I looked at her with panic.

"Cooking? What do you mean he's cooking?" I looked toward the kitchen. I could hear something sizzling. The house smelled like . . . crab. "Ma . . . we have caterers coming."

She was hanging up my coat. "No you don't. They canceled."

"They what?"

"They called about twenty minutes ago. Bupkis. None of their staff can get in with this weather."

I stared at her with a slack jaw.

"It's a good thing your father brought extra food. He thought something like this might happen when that snow rolled in."

"I'm . . . you can't . . ."

"Maggie!" My father's voice rolled out from the kitchen. "Get in here. I need more Old Bay."

I closed my eyes. This was not happening.

Who was I kidding? Of course it was happening.

My mom was heading for the kitchen.

"Hold your horses. Maryann is home."

"She is? *Great*. Yo, Diz," Dad hollered. "Get out here and help your old man. You can make the creamed corn."

Creamed corn?

I wanted to die.

Someone knocked on the front door. Maybe I'd luck out and it would be the Baltimore Police, here to pick me up because Clarissa's bail check bounced.

Nope. It was Christa. She was carrying a huge roasting pan.

"My door is open, letting all my heat out," she said in her thick, German-accented English. "Go over there and bring the rest of the food."

"What food?" I stood back so she could come inside.

"The cabbage and the Kartoffelpuffer. And the Stollen is baking now. It'll be ready in time for dessert."

She pushed past me and headed for the kitchen.

"Christa!" I heard my father bellow. "*Um Himmel's Willen, wie geht's dir?*"

"Ya, you do better to speak English, old man," Christa huffed. "Where you want me to put this goose?"

Goose?

Goose and crab cakes? And creamed corn?

I didn't have to wish for a speedy death. Clarissa would surely take care of it for me.

I followed orders and went next door to schlep back the rest of the food. When I got back to our kitchen with the tray of casseroles, it looked like a bomb had gone off. There wasn't a single surface not covered with Dad's special breading. It was even on the ceiling fan.

My mother pointed toward the back porch.

"Maryann, go out back and help Father Frank with the beer."

She always called my brother Father Frank. And she always called me Maryann. It drove me nuts.

"Frank is here?" I asked. "And *what* beer?"

"He brought a keg of Harp."

"A *keg?* Why the hell did he bring a keg?"

"It was for the Posada celebration tonight at the Knights of Columbus. But that got canceled because of the weather."

"Oh, jeez . . ."

"Go out there and help him get it set up. You know priests aren't any good with hoses."

"Ma . . . we don't *need* beer. We're serving wine and champagne punch."

"You don't drink champagne with crab cakes, Dizzo." My father looked up at me over his vat of goo.

"I could use a pint right now," Christa said.

"Christa's family got stuck in Charlottesville," Ma explained. "This storm is wreaking havoc with everyone's holiday plans."

"Ya, and I had all this food ready." Christa gestured toward her row of dishes. "What am I going to do with a whole goose and all that cabbage?"

I gave up.

"Lemme go help Frank."

I went out back and found my brother ankle deep in the snow piling up on what was supposed to be our patio, trying to tap the keg.

He brightened up at once when he saw me. "Great . . . someone who knows which end is up with these damn things."

"Hey, Frank."

He studied me as we stood together in the swirling snow. "Why so glum?"

I shrugged.

"Diz?"

I looked at him. "Come on, Frank. Look at what's happening here? It's *The Nightmare Before Christmas*—just like I knew it would be."

Frank looked up at the house, then back at me. "What are you talking about?"

"*This.* This weather. This mess." I paused and made air quotes. "Art's Big Ones."

"Oh, I get it. Not the way you wanted to introduce Clarissa's parents to your humble origins?"

"Not really, no."

He smiled at me. "Lighten up, kiddo. It's not that bad."

"Not that bad?" I jerked a thumb toward the house. "Have you seen the kitchen . . . and the ten pounds of red cabbage now congealing in there?"

"Yeah. I heard that K2 and his family got stuck in Virginia. It's wonderful that Christa has your place to come to." He gave me one of his most priestly looks—the ones that took you from unrepentant sinner to postulant in about two-point-four seconds. "No one should be alone on Christmas."

I sighed. He was right. And he knew that I knew he was right.

"Come on," he said. "What's really going on? It's not like you to be this uptight."

I didn't say anything and started working on inserting the hose into the keg.

"Diz?"

I looked up at him.

"Talk to me."

"Aren't you supposed to be off the clock?"

"It's okay. I get double-time for holidays." He smiled.

"I'm just afraid." I didn't see any reason to try to delude him. Besides, even though I thought of myself as a lapsed Catholic, I still knew in my viscera that it wasn't a good idea to lie to a priest—even if he was your brother and you'd shoplifted Milk Duds together as kids.

"Afraid of what?"

I shrugged. "Afraid that if Clarissa's family doesn't like us, she'll come to her senses and go back to her yacht salesman?"

"He didn't sell yachts, he built them."

"Whatever."

"I guess that's it. Sort of. This party is really important to her for some reason. Now it's all gone to hell at light speed." I finished tapping the keg. "We need to prime and test this. Did you bring a cup?"

Frank pulled a ginormous, glass tumbler out of his overcoat pocket and handed it to me.

"Jeez, Frank. Why don't we just use the altar chalice?"

"I left it in my other suit."

I took the glass from him. "Very funny. You should do stand up."

"It's been a while since you've heard one of my homilies, hasn't it?"

"Why do I get the sense that my luck is about to change?"

He laughed.

I siphoned off some of the Harp lager and held it up to examine it. The amber liquid looked glorious against the snowy, gray sky. Oddly, it looked just like Christmas.

"This looks great. I think we're good to go."

"Good. I'm freezing."

"I guess we should go in and get the fireplace going. The way this day is shaping up, we'll be certain to lose power, too."

"One thing before we do . . ."

I sighed. "Okay. Let me have it."

"That's just it, Diz. I don't need to let you have it. You already have it all."

"What are you talking about?"

"You. Clarissa. A houseful of good people who love you."

"Elspeth—"

He held up a hand to stop me. "Elspeth Wiley might be a tad eccentric, but she loves her daughter." He hesitated. "Well . . . maybe not as much as she loves her dog, but she loves her daughter just the same. And her daughter loves you."

"You really think so?"

"You don't?"

I stared down at the snow piling up around my feet. "No. I know she loves me."

"Exactly. Take a minute and just think about where you were

last year at this time. How lonely and desolate. And how did that all end up?"

I looked up at him. "You don't really want me to furnish you with graphic details, do you?"

"No thanks. I have an active imagination."

I shook my head. "I just love her so much, Frank. It scares the shit out of me to think about losing her."

He put a hand on my shoulder. "Then do yourself a favor and quit working so hard to push her away. She has faith in you—and in all of that." He fluttered a gloved hand toward the house. "Borrow a little confidence from her and a little courage from me. I promise it will all work out just fine."

"How can you be so sure?"

He rolled his eyes and yanked open the front of his coat so his collar was plainly visible. "Duh. Connections . . . remember?"

"Oh. Right. He who never sleeps."

"Ain't that the truth? Now let's get back inside and get this party started."

The back door to the house opened and a collision of bright colors filled up the doorway.

"Get in here you two," Ma called out. "Clarissa is home."

I practically swooned. And not from excitement.

"Come on." Frank took hold of my arm. "There is nothing to fear but Dad's creamed corn. The rest will take care of itself." He chuckled. "And eventually, the creamed corn takes care of itself, too."

We trudged our way up the steps and into the house. The short journey felt to me like Napoleon's retreat from Moscow—only I was heading toward the horror, instead of away from it.

When we got inside, I was shocked to see Clarissa standing at the center island in our kitchen and looking over my dad's shoulder at the crab cakes he was forming.

"How much Dijon mustard do you use?" she asked him.

"It depends on how many you're making," he explained. "For this batch, I'm using about a tablespoon. The most important thing is not to use too much filler, and not to pack them together too tightly."

She nodded. "Can I try to make a few?"

I pinched myself and looked around. Had we accidentally walked into someone else's house? Nope. There were our coats and boots lined up in tidy rows near the back door. There was our wine fridge full of Chateau de Nages. There was our kitchen, with its bright red cabinets and tile floor. There was our ceiling fan covered with batter. And there was my dad teaching the love of my life how to make really big crab cakes.

Clarissa looked up and saw Frank and me. Her hundred-watt smile warmed me up from the inside out.

Give light to them that sit in darkness, and in the shadow of death, guide our feet into the way of peace.

Frank would have been proud of my memory.

"Hello you two," she said.

Frank roared across the room and gave her a bear hug. "Hi ya, Red. Nice party."

She hugged him back. "Isn't it? I'm thinking about becoming a full-time event planner." She looked at me. "I think I have a gift for it."

I smiled back at her. "Don't give up your day job just yet."

Ma handed her a bright yellow bistro apron with an enormous cartoon crab stenciled across the front. It read, "I got crabs at Art's" in big, balloon letters. "Here you go, honey. That mess will ruin your cashmere."

Clarissa stepped back from Frank and took the apron from my mother. "Thanks, Maggie."

Maggie?

"So I guess you all did your own introductions?" I asked.

"No." Clarissa was tying on the apron. "Christa introduced us all when I got home."

I looked around. "Where is she?"

Dad pointed toward the common wall our house shared with Christa's. "She went next door to get games for the kids."

"Kids?" I looked at my father with horror. "What kids?"

Clarissa was watching me with an amused expression. "Marty called. Their sitter canceled, so they're bringing the kids."

I was speechless. That was like saying the zombie apocalypse was commencing tonight at our house.

"It ain't Christmas without kids . . . right, Diz?" My father winked at me.

"But . . ." I was practically sputtering. "Your parents?"

Clarissa looked at her watch. "They should be here any minute."

I sagged against the counter. "Oh, god."

"Let me go and try to sweep the steps off again." Frank headed toward the living room.

"Yo, Frank?" Dad called after him. "Put on some music. I put a stack of CDs on top of the stereo."

"Roger, Dad."

A minute later, we heard the deep, smooth tones of Lou Rawls crooning about silver bells.

Clarissa somehow managed to get hold of my hand. She gave my fingers a warm squeeze.

I gave her a grateful look. "I need a drink."

"I can take care of that, Maryann." My mom opened the refrigerator and pulled out a large Rubbermaid pitcher. "I found a great recipe for vegan eggnog. It's surprisingly good . . . you just need to top it off with an extra shot or two of rum."

"Vegan eggnog?" I stared at my mother. "What the hell is that?"

"It's from *Veganomicon*. You make it with almond milk and dates. You blend them all together and add pecans."

I was still confused. "But you're not a vegan." I gestured toward the food strewn around the kitchen. "There's enough dead animal product in here to start a sausage factory."

"Your father has high cholesterol. We're trying to cut back on eggs. And I'm power eating, now. You should try it too. You're looking too pale." She poured two glasses of the frothy mixture and added about four ounces of dark rum to each. I noticed that it didn't sink into the liquid. It floated on the top like an oil slick.

"Good thing he's not worried about his liver," I muttered.

Clarissa kicked me on the shin.

We heard a commotion coming from the living room. Frank ducked his head into the kitchen.

"It's show time. Your parents are here, Red."

Clarissa and I exchanged glances. I dropped my head to her shoulder.

"I don't suppose you'd believe me if I told you I just contracted a virulent case of malaria?"

"Not so much," she said. "Let's go."

She took hold of my hand and pulled me along behind her. We were halfway across the living room before I realized that she was still wearing one of Art's aprons.

"There's my little girl." Bernard Wiley smiled at Clarissa, but quickly did a double take. "I think . . ."

"Hello, Dad. Hello, Mom."

Bernard was helping Elspeth out of her coat. I noticed that she was carrying some kind of bundle—and that the bundle appeared to be . . . whimpering.

Clarissa reached out to take her mother's overcoat and the whimpers gained in intensity. She stepped back and eyed her mother's oddly-shaped bundle with suspicion.

"Please tell me that does not contain what I think it does."

Elspeth Wiley bounced the bundle up and down. "I couldn't leave her at home alone. She's simply too fragile right now."

Clarissa was incredulous. "You brought *Maris* to our party?"

At the mention of its name, a tiny head popped out of its gray fleece overwrap and looked around anxiously. When Maris spotted me, she started growling.

Elspeth glared at me. "However, she might actually have been *safer* at home by herself."

I sighed. "Hello, Mrs. Wiley. It's nice to meet you . . . officially, and, hopefully, under better circumstances."

"That remains to be seen, doesn't it?" She was looking us both up and down. Without her Jackie-O sunglasses, she looked a bit less . . . hysterical. But it seemed pretty clear that Clarissa's dad must have given her the news about us. I half expected her to hand me a restraining order.

Maris was still anxiously scanning the room. I noticed that beneath her blanket she was wearing a black-and-white hounds-tooth check coat. She looked like the Coco Chanel of dogs.

She growled at me again.

It appeared she had about the same disposition, too.

Bernard had more class than I gave him credit for. He stepped into our conversational void and offered me his hand. "Diz, it's great to see you away from the office." He smiled and gave my hand a firm shake. "Thanks for inviting us to your home."

"Believe me, Mr. Wiley," I replied. "It's a pleasure."

Elspeth was sniffing the air in tandem with Maris. I watched their syncopated head bobs and realized that they were dressed alike, too. I wondered if Elspeth and Maris always wore matching outfits? I cut my eyes toward Clarissa, who was eyeing me with an amused expression.

"What is that horrible smell?" Elspeth asked.

I was tempted to tell her that our Glade Plug-In had malfunctioned, but I didn't get the chance.

"Crab cakes," Clarissa replied. "Great ones. I hope you're both hungry."

Elspeth looked at her daughter in horror.

I heard my brother chuckle.

"Forgive my rudeness," I said. "Mr. and Mrs. Wiley, I'd like you to meet my brother, Frank Gillespie." I paused. "But don't be confused when we call him Father."

"You're a priest?" Elspeth asked.

Frank smiled. "It was either that or back-to-back stretches at Leavenworth. Those jumpsuits were a non-starter. Blaze orange has always been a bad color for me, so I opted for the career track that offered a more modest, ecclesiastical palette. Besides, black is so much more slimming, don't you agree, Mrs. Wiley?"

Elspeth and Maris both stared at him with their round dark eyes.

Bernard chuckled. "It's nice to meet you, Frank." They shook hands.

My mom rounded the corner from the kitchen. She was carrying a tray loaded with tumblers containing her vegan eggnog. Each of the glasses was topped with a suspicious-looking puddle of dark brown rum.

"Hello, everyone," Mom called out. "I'm Maryann's mother, Maggie. Come on in and get settled by the fire. We'll have the appetizers ready in a flash."

Appetizers? Oh, yeah. Nothing got a party started like a big bowl of dad's signature, fried globs of creamed corn . . .

Clarissa and I ushered everyone in to the living room.

In fact, the place did look pretty homey and inviting. The gas logs were blazing, and the blue-and-white lights on the Christmas tree were a brilliant complement to the winter storm raging outside. Diana Krall's sexy, jazzy voice was entreating the heavens to let it snow.

Clearly, the heavens had decided to cooperate.

Mom attempted to pass a tumbler of her frothy brew to Elspeth, who recoiled as if the glass contained hemlock.

"I'm lactose intolerant," she explained in a hushed voice.

Mom beamed at her. "Me, too." She handed Elspeth a glass. "Those dairy products cramp me up tighter than a snare drum. You'll love this. It's from *Veganomicon*."

Elspeth's eyes grew wide. "I love that cookbook."

"So do I. But I can't get Maryann's father to try any of the recipes."

"Bernard is the same way. But Maris and I are lacto-ovo-vegetarians."

'It's true." Bernard smiled at us. "I'm an unredeemed flexitarian."

"Here, here." Frank raised his glass in a toast. "Sometimes a man's just gotta have a steak."

Mom hauled a big, leather-covered ottoman over and sat down near Elspeth and Maris. "You two look adorable in those matching jackets. Do you always dress alike?"

Bernard rolled his eyes. "They do lately."

Elspeth shot him a dirty look. "You know that this is part of her recovery therapy."

Mom took the bait . . . of course. "Recovery from what?"

Elspeth leaned closer to her. "Maris is in the throes of an identity crisis."

"Oh, honey, aren't we all?"

"Hers is a response to trauma." She glared at me.

Mom looked confused. "What kind of trauma?"

Elspeth lowered her voice. "Maris thinks she's a Siberian husky."

I choked on my drink. Clarissa patted me between the shoulder blades.

"Maris's entire world was turned topsy turvy by her wild jaunt across Baltimore with that undisciplined hound from hell." Elspeth glowered at me. "Her identity is in shambles. She won't eat. She won't sleep. All she does is whine and stare out the window." She gently stroked Maris's head. "Dr. Finklestein suggested buying her the black-and-white coat as a way for her to access her inner husky."

"Why are you wearing one?" Clarissa asked. "Was there some kind of BOGO sale?"

Bernard chuckled. "Maggie, this is intriguing eggnog. I'm not usually a rum drinker, but this seems to be hitting the spot."

Mom beamed at him. "Let me get us some more." She swiveled around on her ottoman and called out to Dad in the kitchen. "Art! Bring us some more eggnog."

Bernard gave me a quizzical look. "Art?"

I nodded.

"Your father is Art Gillespie?" He pointed at Clarissa's apron. "Back River Art?"

"You know him?" Frank asked.

"Well I'll be damned," a voice bellowed from the doorway. "If it ain't my buddy, Bernie."

Dad set down the pitcher of eggnog and strode across the room to greet Clarissa's dad.

"Artie!" Bernard set down his glass and met Dad halfway. They wrapped each other up in a huge bear hug.

Clarissa and I gaped at them, then at each other. I looked up at Frank.

"I got nothin'." He shrugged.

Dad and Bernie's reunion was interrupted by the thundering sound of footsteps pounding across the front porch.

The door banged open, and Alvin, Simon, and Theodore exploded through it in a swirl of snow like wild winter demons. They spread out across the room like a white stain.

A beleaguered Marty followed behind them.

"Guys . . . boots!" He shook his head and sighed. He saw me and gave me an apologetic look. "Sorry, Diz."

"What about?" I asked.

On the sofa beside Elspeth, Maris bolted upright. She was trembling and staring at the front door.

We heard another rumbling.

Marty raised a hand and rubbed his fingers across his forehead. "This."

There was a blinding flash of something white. Correction. It was a blurry confluence of black-*and*-white. It roared into the room and headed straight for the tray loaded with eggnog.

"Sadie—NO!" Marty yelled.

It was too late.

Sadie knocked Dad's tray to the floor and proceeded to suck up a two-quart pitcher of Mom's vegan concoction.

I heard Elspeth scream. Maris bolted off the sofa and flew across the room to join Sadie.

Marty danced around the two dogs, looking for an opening to reach in and grab the pitcher. It was futile.

"Oh, jeez . . ." Dad looked at me anxiously.

"What is it?" I asked.

"I already pre-loaded it."

Mom slapped him on the arm. "Art. I did, too."

I looked at my glass. "Then why did you add these four-ounce floaters?"

She shrugged. "It looks more authentic."

Elspeth was nearly hysterical. "Maris . . . Maris . . . come to mommy. Turn away from that creature . . ."

It was useless.

"Look at that funny dog dressed like Sadie." Simon was giggling and enjoying the show. Alvin and Teddy didn't notice. They were too busy yanking paper birds off the Christmas tree and throwing them at each other.

"Marty . . ." I began.

"I know, I know," he said. He pulled out a bottle full of bright pink pills from his coat pocket. "Benadryl," he explained. "Works like a charm."

The dogs finished their aperitif and took off for greener pastures.

I was on my feet now.

"Dad? You didn't leave any food out in the kitchen did you?"

"Uh oh," he said.

Bernard held out a hand to stop me. "Let me and Artie take care of this."

Me and Artie? I seriously doubted that Bernard Wiley had ever messed up a dependent clause in his life.

Dad and Bernie disappeared into the kitchen. We all sat there, stupidly, like people at an Irish wake, trying to pretend we weren't hearing the sounds of men shouting, plates crashing, platters clanging, and dog claws scuttling across the tile floor.

Two minutes later, all the noise stopped. An eerie quiet filled up the house.

All except for Vinnie Zummo's bossa nova rendition of "*Noche de Paz.*"

Even the kids noticed.

Bernard emerged from the kitchen with two very subdued dogs heeling at his side.

Marty was incredulous. "How the hell did you manage that?"

Bernard smiled. "I wish I could take credit for it, but thanks are really due to a fifth of Captain Morgan and two pounds of red cabbage."

"Oh, my god." Elspeth was nearly beside herself. "Maris—"

"Is *fine.*" Bernard cut her off. "Look at her. No shakes and no trembles."

"He's right, Mom." Clarissa pointed at the two perfectly composed dogs. "She seems to have made a connection with her inner—and outer—husky."

Maris was pressed up against Sadie. Her black-and-white checked coat looked like a suburb of the larger dog.

"How bad was the damage in the kitchen?" Frank asked.

"Artie already had the crab cakes in the oven," Bernard explained. "Everything other than the cabbage was out of harm's way."

"Two dogs zoned out on rum and red cabbage?" Frank shook his head. "There's gonna be a heartache tonight."

Bernard looked down at them. "I think they'll probably just sleep it off."

The two canine compatriots were starting to look a little unsteady on their feet. Sadie was beginning to sway slightly, and her normally active blue eyes were starting to droop.

127

But Maris looked happy and content—albeit sleepy.

"There is a god after all," I quipped.

"Yo, Diz. I'm really sorry about bringing her along, too." Marty was scooping up the paper birds his kids had flung around the room. "But we couldn't leave her at home alone."

"It's okay, Marty."

"I mean, the last time we tried that, she ate nine of those jumbo-sized boxes of Fruity Pebbles."

I held up a palm. "It's really okay, Marty."

"Sheila got them on sale at Costco."

"Marty . . ."

"Sadie shit a rainbow for a week."

"It's really *okay*, Marty. You can stop apologizing."

The front door banged open, and Christa and Sheila walked in.

I sighed and leaned into Clarissa. "Why don't we just take that damn thing off its hinges?"

"My, god. It's practically whiteout conditions out there." Sheila was carrying a stack of board games. "Where do you want me to plant the munchkins?"

Frank stood up. "I'm on it. Let me take them to Diz's office." He turned around and addressed the kids. "Come on, you scalawags. Let's go play some cutthroat Candyland."

Sheila looked at him gratefully. "You're a saint, Father Frank."

Frank winked at her. "From your mouth to god's ear, Sister Sheila." He took off with the three boys in tow. I noticed that Marty passed him the bottle of bright pink pills.

"They usually don't make it past Gum Drop Mountain, if you get my drift," he whispered.

Frank shook the bottle like a rattle. "Who wants some chocolate milk?"

"We do!" the kids screamed in unison.

"Where should I put the Stollen?" Christa was holding a cookie sheet covered with a striped dishtowel.

Bernard jerked a thumb toward the kitchen. "Someplace high."

Christa looked down at the two swaying canines.

"Ya, well it looks like the Stollen won't be the only thing high

128

around here." She looked up at Bernard. "What's wrong with the Hündinnen?"

"It's complicated," Bernard explained.

"They're drunk." My dad emerged from the kitchen. "Christa, meet Clarissa's father, Bernie Wiley. The lovely woman on the sofa is his wife, Elspeth." He pointed down at Maris. "This is their prized Whippet, Maris."

Christa looked back and forth between Maris and Elspeth. "*Mein, gott. Weibliche Zwillinge.*"

Bernard chuckled. "I think these two need to lie down."

He crossed to the fireplace. The two dogs staggered along beside him. Elspeth jumped up and spread Maris's gray fleece blanket out in front of the hearth. Sadie and Maris collapsed on top of it, wrapped around each other like Chinese nesting dolls.

"They do look pretty happy," Elspeth observed. "Maybe Dr. Finklestein was right about immersion therapy . . ."

Dad clapped his hands together. "All the food is ready. How about we fix our plates and eat in here by the fire?"

"Shouldn't we wait for the other guests to arrive?" I asked.

"There aren't any other guests." Clarissa looked at me. "Everyone we invited is here."

"What are you talking about?" I was confused. "You said you were inviting twenty other people?"

She shook her head.

"I don't get it."

"I know you don't. I wanted this to just be a family event, but I knew you'd never agree to it." She gestured toward the room. "And here they all are." She smiled at me. "Our blended family."

"But the caterers . . ."

"There are no caterers. I asked your father to do the food."

I looked up at Dad. "You knew about this?"

He nodded. "Sorry for the deception, Dizzo. It was supposed to be a surprise."

It was a surprise all right.

"Well, I, for one, am glad about that." Bernard emptied his tumbler of eggnog. "I've been a fan of Artie's crab cakes forever."

129

"I was going to ask how you two knew each other." I felt like I was sleepwalking.

"Oh, that's easy. I have my boat worked on at a place in Essex. I found Art's Back River Crab House years ago." Bernard looked at his wife. "They're the best crab cakes on the Eastern shore."

Elspeth rolled her eyes. "Now I know why none of your pants fit any more."

Dad nodded. "Bernie's photo is on my wall of shame."

Bernie ate one of Dad's big ones?

"Did you know about this?" I asked Clarissa.

"Nope." She bumped my shoulder. "It's a Christmas miracle."

"You can say that again."

"Speaking of Christmas miracles . . ." Frank reappeared from the hallway that led to my office. "The three little kings are already passed out."

"No way." Marty pumped a fist in the air. "It usually takes longer than this for the Benadryl to kick in."

Sheila looked at him in horror. "Benadryl?"

He nodded. "Yeah. I gave some to Father Frank to help speed things along."

"Marty, you asshole."

"What?" He held out both hands. "You always do."

"Right," she said. "And I *did* . . . right before we left home."

Marty looked at Frank. "Uh oh."

"How many milligrams are the tablets?" Elspeth asked.

"Twenty-five," Sheila replied. "I gave them each one."

"I gave them each one more," Frank added.

Elspeth did a quick calculation. "That's two times the suggested dosage for children under age twelve, but they appear to be exceptionally . . . well fed. So they should fare just fine. However, I wouldn't expect them to wake up any time soon."

I gave Clarissa a confused look.

"My mother is an expert on prescription drugs," she explained.

"Well, merry Christmas, one and all." Marty suddenly looked more relaxed than I'd ever seen him. He collapsed into a chair. "Can a fella get anything to drink around here?"

"Want a beer?" Frank asked.

"God, yes."

"I'm on it. Anyone else?" Frank looked about the room. Heads nodded all around. Even Elspeth timidly raised her hand.

Clarissa eyed her mother with surprise.

"What?" Elspeth waved her off. "I like a cold one from time to time."

Clarissa leaned into me. "I'm pretty sure I'm having an out-of-body experience."

I squeezed her hand. "That makes two of us."

Christa walked in from the kitchen. She handed Frank an oversized glass pitcher.

"Use this. It'll save you a few trips."

"Good idea." Frank took the pitcher and headed for the back door.

"How about that food?" Dad clapped his hands together again. "Come on, everyone. Let's hit the kitchen and fix our plates."

Everyone got up and followed Dad and Christa. Clarissa and I stayed behind. We sat for a minute, listening to the clatter of plates and silverware, punctuated by laughter and snippets of light-hearted conversation.

It the streetlight outside the front windows, we could see the snow coming down harder than ever.

Maris snorted in her sleep and scrunched in closer to Sadie.

Vinnie Zummo had finished his set. Mel Torme was now singing "The Christmas Song."

Clarissa rested her red head on my shoulder. I wrapped an arm around her.

"This is what I always wanted," she muttered.

"What?" I was tempted to ask if she meant a drug-induced holiday. I wondered if Frank still had that bottle of pink pills handy . . .

"This," she said. "A house full of noisy, happy people. Coats piled on the bed. Kids sleeping down the hall." She kissed me on the neck. "You."

I did what I always did when Clarissa kissed me. I forgot about everything else but her. The dogs, the kids, the crab cakes and cabbage, the winter storm socking us all in—everything receded into the background. Even my burgeoning police record seemed insignificant compared to the heady rush of heat and happiness I experienced when she was this close to me. I hoped it would always be this way for us.

I smiled into her hair.

If we could survive a night like this one, I was pretty sure the odds were stacking up in our favor.

"I love you," I said.

"You'd better." She pushed something into my hand.

"What's this?" I looked down at the small, red box.

"Remember I told you I had one thing to take care of before I came home tonight?"

I nodded.

"I took care of it."

My heart was pounding. Even though I was pretty sure what the box contained, I was having a hard time taking it in.

"Is this what I think it is?"

She shrugged. "It depends."

I turned the box over in my shaking hands. "On?"

"On whether you think it's the ridiculously plainest, solid platinum ring Cartier ever hammered out. If so, you'd be within spitting distance of right."

I was speechless.

She leaned into me. "It's legal in Maryland now, you know."

I nodded.

"You wanna try it on and see if it fits?"

I nodded again. My throat was thick.

"Diz?"

I looked at her with my heart in my eyes.

"Merry Christmas."

I leaned in to kiss her, and there was a roar of applause from the kitchen doorway.

We grinned at each other and touched our foreheads together like the guilty, happy women in love we were. Then we got up and joined our blended family in a curiously epicurean feast that would forever be the stuff of Christmas legend.

(plus one)

T'was the Nightmare
Before Christmas

It. Wasn't. My. Fault.

Somehow, these four words were becoming a leitmotif for me.

Lately, I'd said them so many times that I considered having them tattooed on my forehead. That way, they could just precede me into every situation where they'd later have relevance.

But this mess?

This was one for the record books. If Guinness had a category for "most consecutive Christmas holidays blown completely to smithereens," I'd be their poster child.

But did I ever get *my* day in court? Did I ever get a chance to tell *my* side of the story? Was I ever regarded as *innocent* until proven guilty?

No. Not by the redheaded Lord Chancellor who presided like a thundercloud over every case of *Crown v. Gillespie.*

In fact, Clarissa is what they used to call a "hanging judge." Which means that whenever I get hauled up before her to face charges for some new crime against nature, she just sighs and starts looking around for a sturdy tree limb.

This time was no exception.

It all started yesterday when Marty ducked his sweaty head into my cubicle at work, and told me he wasn't feeling well. I wasn't really surprised by that announcement. It was our last working day before Christmas, and we'd just had our annual office potluck luncheon where Marty had distinguished himself by ingesting his weight in Vienna sausages and cream-of-something casseroles. It didn't help matters that those nimrods from the mailroom added so much rum to the bowl of eggnog that it took on the consistency of Kutzit varnish remover.

It tasted like it, too.

I managed to exercise more restraint that Marty did, however, and it seemed clear that he was on the verge of paying the price for his excesses.

"Yo, Diz? I think I'm gonna hurl."

"Great." I said. "You came in here to tell me that?"

"No. I came in here because I need a ride home."

"Now?" I looked down at my desk. I was only halfway through fact-checking Grover Westlake's diatribe about the proposed development of bike shares, a barge pool and a bridge connecting the east and west sides of the Inner Harbor. It was all part of his year-end "Best of Baltimore" column, and the draft was due back to editorial by three-thirty. "I can't leave now, man. I gotta finish this article."

"Dude." Marty leaned against the doorway of my cubicle. His face had an odd pallor—vaguely like the color of that eggnog. "I'm not kidding...I think I'm gonna..."

He clapped a hand to his mouth.

Oh, Judas.

I grabbed my trashcan and thrust it toward him. Marty bent over and let it fly. It was pretty impressive. His retching went on and on. As disgusting as it was, I was surprised to notice that the partly ingested casseroles looked just about the same as they all had before the luncheon commenced.

I was relieved that, for once, I'd listened to Clarissa, and steered clear of any dish that appeared to contain mayonnaise as its primary ingredient.

Marty had finished his unpleasant errand and dropped down onto a chair.

"God." He was wiping his mouth on the sleeve of his shirt.

"Are you all right?"

He gave me a miserable look. "Do I look all right?"

He offered me the trashcan.

I recoiled. "No thanks. You can keep it."

"I need to go home," he repeated. "You can drive me and drop the van off later."

"Right." I nodded.

Marty was flying solo this week. His wife, Sheila, was in Michi-

136

gan, helping her mother convalesce after undergoing emergency quintuple bypass surgery. How Marty was managing on his own to wrangle all three of their kids and that demon dog was beyond me.

I didn't want to think too much about it.

"Let me call upstairs, and we'll head out."

He gave a weary-looking nod and tugged the trashcan closer. I took that as a bad sign.

Clarissa answered on the first ring.

"Wylie."

"Hey, honey, it's me."

Marty started retching again. I turned away from him and lowered my voice. "I have a bit of a situation down here."

"What is that ungodly noise?"

Clarissa always cut to the chase.

"It's Marty."

"Of *course* it is." She sighed. "What's wrong?"

"He's sick. I need to run him home."

"Sick? What kind of sick?"

I looked over my shoulder at Marty.

Uh oh.

"The kind of sick that means if I don't soon get him outta here, Wylie Magazine Group is gonna have to invest in a butt load of new trashcans."

"Oh, god. Okay...*go.* But don't forget that dad is dropping Maris off at five-thirty."

Maris was her mother's neurotic whippet. Clarissa's parents were spending Christmas in Old Quebec this year, which meant we'd be stuck taking care of Maris for the holidays. My parents had already decamped for a weeklong, canasta-thon in Boca. Thank god my mother took her four cats along.

"I won't forget," I assured her. "But right now, I need your help with something."

"What is it?" Her voice was tinged with suspicion.

"My Grover Westlake article is only about two-thirds finished."

"When's it due?"

I looked at my watch. "In about ninety minutes."

She sighed. "Have Susan send it up. I'll take care of it."

"Thanks, baby. See you later."

"Diz?" Clarissa asked.

"Yeah?"

"Take care of Marty, but be sure to douse yourself liberally with Purel before you set foot inside our house."

"Yes, dear."

"I love you."

I smiled. Even with the great distraction of Marty, heaving his guts out in the corner behind me, I couldn't help feeling all the ways her simple declaration filled my world up with light.

"I love you, too."

She hung up.

I turned around to face Marty. In the sixty seconds I'd been on the phone, he'd gone downhill pretty rapidly. He was sweating profusely and his pallor had gone from gray to green.

"Can you make it to the parking deck?" I asked.

He nodded. "But I'm gonna need another one of these." He indicated the trashcan.

I grabbed my coat. "We'll figure something out."

❈ ❈ ❈

By my calculation, Marty threw up at least four more times on the drive home. It was unclear to me whether or not these bouts were what you'd call *productive*—but it was an impressive performance just the same.

"Dude?" I asked after the second or third episode. "How many of those Vienna sausages did you eat?"

We were crawling along East Pratt Street. I had both of the front windows down. It was cold as hell and spitting snow, but without the fresh air blowing through the van's passenger compartment, the stench would've been unbearable.

Marty groaned and hunched over the hefty bag we snagged from the canteen on our way out of the building.

Again?

I don't want to suggest here that I didn't care about Marty's distress. I did. But I guess I had enough of a Puritan streak to believe that he was reaping the rewards of the loutish behavior he'd exhibited by scarfing up so much bad food at the luncheon.

And, selfishly, I was eager to get on with my own plans for the holiday. For the first time since we'd been together, Clarissa and I were planning a quiet, just us kind of Christmas. That meant no company, no family drama, no storm-of-the-century weather events, no marauding, psychotic dogs, no restraining orders, and, hopefully, no jail time for me.

Just us. *Alone.* We'd been planning it for most of the month.

Well…we'd have Maris. But we had a plan for that…we'd just double up on her doses of puppy Xanax to keep her in a chemically induced state of bliss.

Yep. We'd be at home together, enjoying our own quiet rendition of a sweeter, simpler, Currier and Ives kind of Christmas.

Except for the food.

We'd spent every evening for the last week, pouring over our dog-eared copy of *Mastering The Art of French Cooking*, looking for exactly the right dish to prepare on Christmas day. And, finally, we found it. Roast goose with a chestnut and prune stuffing, finished with a brandy-based sauce. To drink, we were recreating Paul Child's signature reverse martini: French vermouth, Dubonet, orange essence and dark rum.

I could taste it all right now….

Marty retched into the trash bag. Again.

Okay. Maybe not *now*…but I knew it was all going to be extraordinary.

And the best part? We were planning our wedding. *Our wedding.*

We decided months ago that we would short circuit all the family hoopla and sneak off to City Hall tonight—Christmas Eve. Just the two of us. My brother, Father Frank, would be our only witness.

We'd hatched this plan because it became clear to us in short order that trying to orchestrate an event that could balance the Wylie family need for refinement with the Gillespie family need for crab claws and creamed corn would surely generate chaos on an apocalyptic scale. Although Clarissa did wryly suggest that it was too bad film director

Robert Altman died. In her view, he would have made the perfect wedding planner.

So here I was, six hours and change away from the happiest night of my life, and my best friend was heaving his guts out in the middle of a traffic jam on St. Paul Street.

I inched the van windows up a notch.

It looked like the weather was taking a nosedive, too. What started out as "scattered flurries" was starting to resemble a bona fide snow squall.

I didn't like the way these odds were starting to stack up. An unhappy thought occurred to me. I looked at Marty.

"Um...who's taking care of the kids?"

He fixed me with a bleary-eyed gaze, but didn't say anything.

"Marty? Dude...please. Tell me you have somebody lined up to help you."

He shook his head.

I felt myself beginning to sweat. *Dear god, this was not happening.*

"Marty?"

"It should...only...be for...one night."

One night? One night with Alvin, Simon, and Theodore?

I'd rather shove a hot poker into my eye.

Another horrifying prospect reared its ugly head.

"What about...*her?*" I asked.

"Who?" Marty looked confused. And green. Very, very green.

"That servant of Cerberus you call a dog."

"Oh. Yeah," he said. You'll need to take Sadie, too."

Make that hot pokers in both eyes.

"You can't be serious?"

"Do I not *look* serious?" Marty bent over and retched into the bag, just for emphasis.

Oh, god. Clarissa was going to kill me....

Someone blew a car horn and I jumped about a foot into the air. *Shit.* I was so lost in contemplating my misfortunes that I didn't notice traffic had started moving again. I hit the gas and the van lurched forward.

Bad idea. Marty all but did a face plant into his hefty bag.

Okay, I reasoned. *It was only for one night. With luck this…thing…*
Marty had would be over with in about eight hours, and hell could go back
into its box.

He was retching again.

Make that twelve hours….

❈ ❈ ❈

"You have to make Teddy wear his retainer."

"Right."

"He won't want to. He'll try to hide it and say it's lost."

"Okay."

"Last night, he hid it in Alvin's Pull-Ups."

"Pull-Ups. Check."

"The dirty ones."

I looked up from my notepad. *Dirty ones?*

"Gross."

"Tell me about it. Alvin's had the trots for three days. I had to soak
the retainer in Clorox."

"Good god."

"Now Teddy *really* hates it."

Marty was on his knees, hugging the commode in their master
bathroom. I was taking notes.

"And he has to have ear drops twice a day."

"Ear drops. Roger."

"*Twice* a day, Diz. I'm not kidding. Otherwise he gets this smelly,
yellow ear magma that oozes out and stains everything."

I made the note. "Twice a day. Right."

"And you have to take them to see Santa Claus tonight."

I lowered the notepad. "Marty…."

He held up a hand. "I *promised* them, Diz. It's their last chance
before Christmas."

I sighed and looked at my watch.

It was nearly two-thirty. I still had to pack up all their shit and
then go and retrieve them from their after school program at Church
of the Redeemer on Charles Street.

141

And I had to be home by five-thirty to meet Bernard Wiley for the Maris handoff.

"Can't they just skip it this year?"

"Sure." Marty groaned and rested his head on the porcelain rim. "They probably won't scream for more than six hours...seven, tops. Of course, Alvin starts projectile vomiting when he cries for more than ten minutes."

My shoulders drooped. "Santa Claus. Check."

"Sadie has to be crated at night."

Crated?

I looked at him. "What kind of crate?"

"You know." He waved a hand. "A *crate*. With bars and shit."

That sounded about right. If I had *my* way, Sadie would be spending Christmas in Leavenworth.

"I don't have one of those. Can I take yours?"

"If you can get it apart."

"How big is it?"

"About the size of a Buick."

Okay, so that wasn't happening. "I'll figure something else out."

"Yeah, well make sure you do. She eats upholstery."

Marty was fading. I needed to get him up and into bed. "Come on. Let's get you settled."

I helped him stand up and guided him into the bedroom. He'd already shucked off most of his clothes as soon as we got inside the house. I helped him crawl beneath the covers.

"Do you have food?" I asked.

He moaned.

"Okay. Forget about food. Do you have juice? Gatorade?"

"I don't want anything. I just want to *die*."

"Right." I pulled the covers up to his chin. "Your cell phone is right here on the nightstand. You call me if you need anything, okay?"

He nodded and closed his eyes.

"I'll call Sheila for you."

He grunted.

I was halfway out of the room when I heard him call out to me. I paused in the doorway.

"What did you say?"

"Presents," he muttered.

I took a step back into the room. "What presents?"

"For the kids. They're in the back of the van, beneath two, forty-pound bags of cedar chips."

"You mean their Christmas presents?"

He nodded. "They're not wrapped...."

I opened my mouth to protest, but it was useless. He had already dropped off to sleep.

I did the best I could trying to collect everything I thought we'd need to manage the kids for a night. I just grabbed clothes, jammies, and stuffed animals and crammed them all into a couple of pillowcases. Fortunately, toothbrushes, medicines, and Teddy's retainer were all on a shelf in their bathroom. And Marty was right...that thing did smell like Clorox.

I also grabbed a big, open box of Pull-Ups.

As soon as I started down the stairs, I heard a high-pitched wailing sound that was like fingernails on a chalkboard.

Sadie. The Siberian Vortex.

Let the games begin.

❧ ❧ ❧

I still don't know how I managed to get all three kids strapped into their car seats after I picked them up at day care.

Who designs those contraptions, anyway? They're like straight jackets in Day-Glo colors.

Sadie was riding shotgun up front. I had to tie her into the passenger seat with bungee cords so she wouldn't make a break for it when I got out to get the kids.

"Where's daddy?" Simon asked.

Alvin and Theodore seemed too preoccupied with trying to figure out why Sadie was strapped into the front seat to notice that I was the one picking them up.

I lifted Simon into the van.

"He's sick today, and he asked me to come and pick you guys up."

"Why is Sadie in the front seat?" Alvin asked. "I have to pee," he added, before I could reply.

"You have to pee?" I looked back at the church. "Didn't you go inside?"

He nodded. "But Brian Plotnik pushed me outta the way and I didn't get to finish it."

Theodore had already climbed into the van by himself. He strapped himself into his car seat so fast his little hands were a blur.

"Brian Plotnik hates you," he said to his brother. "I hate you, too." Alvin started to cry. He was holding his crotch with both hands.

Great. Now what was I supposed to do?

I looked around for someone to ask for help. People were fleeing the scene like inmates in the aftermath of a prison break. Nobody would even make eye contact with me.

"Okay, guys. I'm going to lock the doors on the van while I take Alvin back inside to use the bathroom. You have to *promise* me that you won't open the doors for anyone until I get back. Okay?"

They both nodded.

"You have to promise…cross your hearts."

They looked at each other.

"Well?" I asked.

"We don't know what that means," Simon said.

I sighed. "It means that if you promise not to open the doors, no matter what, I'll take you to Dairy Queen on the way home."

Their eyes lit up.

"We promise!" they cried in unison.

"Okay." I slid the side door closed and hit the lock button on the key fob.

I looked down at Alvin, who was now crouching by the curb.

Uh oh.

A wet stain was making determined progress down the inside of his pant leg. A small lake spread out beneath his Spider Man sneakers. Steam rose up around his little feet like an acrid cloud.

"Dude…."

"I had to go," he cried. "I *told* you."

I sighed. At least I had some clean clothes with me. He could

144

change once I got him inside, and I could wash the soiled stuff when I got them home.

"It's okay," I said to Alvin. "I'm not mad at you. I have some dry clothes for you in the van."

I hit the door unlock button on the key fob. Nothing happened. I hit it again. Zilch.

Great.

"Hey, guys?" I tapped on the side window. "Wanna open the door?"

They ignored me.

I tapped again—louder this time.

"Simon? Teddy? Open the door, please."

They continued to ignore me. I did notice, however, that Sadie was staring at me with her clear, blue eyes. "Good luck with this one," her gaze seemed to say.

I slapped the side panel with the flat of my hand. "Boys? This isn't funny. I know you hear me. Open the door."

Nothing.

Alvin started to cry again.

Judas.

"Simon and Theodore? I'm *not* kidding. Open this door right now."

Silence.

Enlightenment dawned. I decided to try another approach.

"Okay, boys. I'm *very* proud of you both. You passed the test. Now open the door, and I'll let you order whatever you want at Dairy Queen."

The door locks shot up with a resounding thunk.

I was proud of my ingenuity. Even Sadie looked impressed.

"Come on, Alvin." I rolled open the door and lifted him into the van. "Let's get you into some dry pants."

"I want a Peanut Buster Parfait," Simon said.

"I want a Dilly Bar," Teddy added.

"Can Sadie have a puppy cup?" Simon asked.

I was trying to find a pair of pants that would fit Alvin. His shoes were soaked, too—and smelly.

"What's a puppy cup?" I asked.

Sadie chose this moment to begin singing the songs of her people.

145

It wasn't exactly howling. It was more like…yodeling. *Loud* yodeling. Loud, *endless* yodeling.

"What's the matter with her?" I shouted above the din.

Simon yelled back. "She wants a puppy cup."

Right. *Of course she does.*

I had forty-five minutes to roar through the drive-in at Dairy Queen and get home in time to meet Bernard and Maris. I wondered if Dairy Queen had a dirty, double Goose martini on the drive-through menu?

I gave up on finding Alvin a pair of pants that would fit. I pulled out a pair of pajama bottoms.

"Here, buddy. Let's put these on."

"Those aren't mine," he complained. "They're Teddy's."

"Gross!" Teddy yelled. "Don't let him pee on my pajamas."

"He's not going to pee on anybody's pajamas." I looked at Alvin. "Are you?"

He took a minute to think about it.

"Dude?" I asked again.

He shook his head. *Thank god.* I got the dry pants on him and strapped him into his car seat. Sadie was still yodeling at ear-splitting decibel levels when I climbed behind the wheel.

"How do we get her to stop?" I shouted at the boys.

"Mommy usually just turns the radio up really loud," Simon said.

Okay. That might work. I started the van and turned on the radio. Polka music came blasting out of the speakers. It sounded like a medley from *The Best of Myron Florin.*

Miraculously, Sadie shut up. Immediately. Then she resumed looking placidly out the passenger window.

Whatever. I shook my head and pulled the van out into traffic.

❀ ❀ ❀

Clarissa wasn't buying it.

"Explain to me again why we have a house full of screaming children?" She plucked a furry, gray and white tumbleweed up off the hardwood floor. "And dog hair?"

"The dog hair is *not* my fault." I felt confident enough to try and acquit myself of that offense.

Sadie decided that this was a perfect moment to bolt across the room at a full lope. She slid to halt just inches short of the Christmas tree, where Maris was reposing on a fluffy, red pillow. I noticed that she was carrying something in her mouth, but I was too preoccupied with mounting my defense to pay much attention to it.

"As you can see," I continued. "Not all of the dog hair is my fault."

Clarissa dropped her hand. "Nice try."

"Come on, Clar. What was I supposed to do? Call the National Guard? He's *really* sick."

She closed her eyes and let out a deep sigh.

I put an arm around her shoulders and pulled her closer. "It's only for one night."

She slowly shook her head.

I kissed her hair.

I honestly thought we were home free until Teddy decided to create a makeshift trap set out of our pots and pans. He was no Art Blakey, but to be fair, he was doing a credible job keeping up with the *Retro Cool Bossa Nova Christmas* CD I had playing in the background.

Clarissa looked toward the kitchen, then back at me. "That," she pointed a finger toward Teddy and his stainless steel skins, "I can't even talk about. But explain to me why we're still listening to this awful music."

I was offended. "It's Vinnie Zummo."

"I *know* who it is."

"You don't like it?"

"I wouldn't go that far," she explained. "Let's just say that any traces of nuance or quirky appeal it had for me evaporated after the first five-hundred times you played it."

"*They* like it." I gestured toward the dogs. They were curled up together on the big red pillow, happily munching away on something.

I took a closer look.

Uh oh.

"Excuse me."

I disengaged myself and walked over to retrieve what was left of the whole pork tenderloin I had taken out of the fridge when we got home.

There wasn't much.

I held up the soggy, plastic wrapper.

"I guess we're eating out?"

"What *is* that?" Clarissa had a horrified expression on her face.

"It *was* a pork tenderloin. It was going to be our dinner."

"You left meat out on the counter?" Clarissa was incredulous.

"*No*. It was on top of the fridge." I looked at Sadie, who was gazing back at me with her pale eyes. "How did I know this dog was part Flying Wallenda?"

"Diz...." Clarissa started to say something but thought better of it. It was clear that another thought had occurred to her. "Aren't there supposed to be *three* of them?" She looked around the living room.

"Three of what?"

She rolled her eyes. "Children. Three children."

"Yeah...."

"So where are the other two?"

Shit.

"Um." I raised my eyes. "Upstairs?"

Clarissa took off her coat and calmly draped it over the back of the sofa. "Why don't you go and check? I'll stay here and guard the perimeter."

"Right."

I took the stairs two at a time.

Sure enough, Alvin and Simon were in our room playing. Sort of.

Alvin had pulled every pair of Clarissa's shoes out of the closet and appeared to be trying them all out. Right now, he was striding back and forth in a pair of sling-back Jimmy Choo's.

Oddly, I thought they had a slenderizing effect on him.

Simon was stretched out on our bed with what was left of his Peanut Buster Parfait, watching TV. I was impressed that he figured out how to navigate his way through all five of the remotes it took just to turn the damn thing on.

He was watching *BBC World News*.

I tried to ignore the chocolate stains on the bolster.

"Come on, guys." I clapped my hands together. "It's time to go see Santa."

That got their attention. Alvin made a dash for the door, which was pretty impressive considering his footwear. I caught him by the back of his sweatshirt as he flew past me.

"Hold up there, Hoss. Let's change our shoes."

"He's a pervert," Simon chimed in from the bed.

"Hey." I held up a finger. "That's not a very nice thing to say. Lots of people like fancy shoes."

Simon was now flipping channels. He stopped on the Bloomberg channel. Charlie Rose was interviewing Anthony Bourdain.

"He's wearing a pair of your underwear, too," he added.

"My..." I looked toward my dresser. Several of the drawers were standing open and clothes were strewn across the carpet.

I looked down at Alvin. He gazed back at me with his wide, dark eyes.

"I hope you picked the boxer shorts. Those briefs tend to creep up on you after a while."

He nodded.

"Come on. Let's get your shoes.

❋ ❋ ❋

Santa's Crystal Snow Palace was unfortunately situated smack dab in the middle of Towson Town Center mall. It was a twenty-five minute drive under the best circumstances, but tonight wasn't remotely like the best circumstances. It was the night before Christmas, and two-thirds of the population of Baltimore was out cramming all of the highways and byways in last-minute shopping frenzies. The aggregate lack of enthusiasm for these endeavors was evident in the general absence of driving courtesies.

People were cranky, in a hurry, and eager to be anyplace but in their cars stuck in holiday traffic.

The boys were all strapped securely into their car seats. Clarissa seemed to have greater facility navigating the mechanics of those than I did. In retrospect, that shouldn't really have surprised me. I recalled watching her truss a goose once. It was hypnotic—and it was the only reason I consented to try another one for this year's Christmas dinner. She did it so quickly and easily that I had to wonder about where she acquired such a skill. It sure didn't seem like anything she'd have picked up at Princeton. But I reasoned that since she'd always had an uncanny ability to tie my ass up in knots, this probably was just the logical extension of a natural talent.

The biggest hurdle we had to navigate in preparation for tonight's great, unplanned Santa pilgrimage—after we got everyone to pee… *twice*…was what to do with the dogs.

The dogs.

Not since "Ted Cruz" had any pair of words filled me with so much dread, and the promise of certain disaster.

We went back and forth about what to do with them while we were out of the house. Clarissa seemed content to lock them up on the back porch. Maris had arrived with her customary bevy of cashmere winter coats, so she'd be fine in the crisp night air for a couple of hours. Sadie, on the other hand, had fur that was thick enough to attract hunters and trappers from the Yukon.

Still, I worried about the wisdom of leaving the Harry Houdini of dogs alone in a largely unsecured enclosure.

Where was razor wire when you needed it?

Salvation arrived in the form of Christa Schröder, my German neighbor. Her son, Karl, was arriving tomorrow to take her back to North Carolina to spend the rest of the holiday with him, his wife Maisy, and their four children. Christa had been baking all day to prepare for the trip. She appeared at our door just as we had about decided that our safest option was to take the dogs along with us. She was bearing a fresh loaf of Stollen. She thrust the hot, sweet bread into my hands and bent down to coo at the dogs, who were dancing around her feet like puppies.

"My precious beauties." She wrapped them both up in her large arms. "What bundles of joy are."

Clarissa and I exchanged glances.

Christa was now softly singing to the dogs in German.

"Um. Christa?" I asked.

She looked up at me with her sky blue eyes. Incredibly, the dogs were already half asleep.

"Ya?" she asked.

I gestured toward the boys, who were watching the spectacle with as much amazement as the two of us.

"Marty is sick and we have his kids. We're just heading out to take them to see Santa Claus. Would you mind watching the dogs for us? It should only be for a couple of hours."

"Sure." She waved a hand toward the wall that separated our row houses. "I can feed them some schnitzel." She dropped her gaze back to the dogs. "You would like that, wouldn't you, my pretties?"

Problem solved. If we played our cards right, maybe Christa would offer to keep them overnight, too. It was Christmastime, after all. Miracles were to be expected.

We'd finally reached the turnoff for Towson Town Center. Clarissa gasped when she got a look at the parking lot.

"This looks worse than Epcot Center on the fourth of July."

I tried to put a positive spin on it. "It's not that bad. I bet we find something close to the entrance."

Fat chance. There were long lines of cars trolling bumper-to-bumper in a hunt for any sliver of car-sized space. We crawled around for about ten minutes. The snow was still coming down, and the big, fat flakes swirled around in the beams from the headlights. It was like watching an epic pillow fight at the North Pole.

"I think we should give this up."

I glanced over at Clarissa. "We can't. We have to take the kids to see Santa."

"Not that." She met my eyes. "*This.* We're never going to find a space in here."

"What do you think we should do?"

"Get out of this maze and head over to Goucher College. We can park in one of their lots."

"Won't we get towed?"

"The day before Christmas? I doubt it."

I sighed. "Even if I can succeed in getting us out of here before Epiphany—which right now looks extremely unlikely—how on earth will going over there help us? We can't walk that far with the kids."

Clarissa held up her cell phone.

"We won't be walking. I'll get us an Uber."

An Uber?

"My god. You're brilliant."

She smiled at me.

"And gorgeous. Have I told you that lately?"

"Gross."

I looked in the rearview mirror. Simon was staring back at us.

"You guys should get a room," he added.

"Hey, wise guy." I wagged a finger at him. "We *have* a room. And if memory serves, you were pretty comfortable in there just about an hour ago. So mind your P's and Q's."

"What-*ever*." He looked down at his electronic Sudoku game.

"I'm hungry." Teddy kicked the back of my seat.

"I know, dude. So am I. We'll stop for some dinner after we see Santa."

"I wouldn't count on it," Clarissa muttered.

"What do you mean?" I was piloting the van down one of the long avenues that led to the Goucher campus.

"Did you see the lines of people outside all those restaurants?"

"I have to pee." Alvin decided to join the conversation.

Clarissa swiveled around on her seat and glared at him. "Don't. Even. Think. About. It."

"Dude," Simon chimed in. "If I were you, I'd hold it."

"Cross your legs," Teddy added.

I turned into the visitor lot. "Where should we park?"

Clarissa pointed at a white vehicle parked beneath a streetlight. It seemed to blend into the snow flying around it. "How about right beside that?"

"The minivan?"

She nodded. "It's our Uber."

"You got us a minivan?"

"Of course. Kids. Car seats." She held up her cell phone. "It's called UberFAMILY."

I was amazed. "I didn't even think of that."

"They did a feature about this last week on Bloomberg," Simon volunteered. "I predict it will go public before the end of the second quarter. You heard it here first."

I looked at Clarissa and jerked a thumb toward the back seat. "Is this kid really Marty's?"

"It does beg the question," she agreed.

"Okay." I put the van in park. "Let's offload and get this show on the road."

Within ten minutes, we were all crammed inside our Uber, and navigating our way back to Towson Town Center mall. The driver dropped us off at the entrance closest to Santa's Crystal Snow Palace. I think he took pity on us. It was pretty clear that we were completely out of our league with this errand.

"You folks don't really have kids, do you?" he asked, after watching us struggle to get all three of the boys back out of his van.

"What tipped you off?" I was sucking on the tip of the thumb I had nearly pinched off while trying to unsnap Alvin's seatbelt.

"Call it a hunch," he said. He looked at Clarissa. "Look. We're really not supposed to do this, but how about you just give me a call on my cell when you're ready to head back to your car?" He handed her a slip of paper.

Clarissa took it from him. "Thank you, but how do you know you'll be available when we're through?"

"You're taking them to see Santa, right?"

She nodded.

"At seven o'clock on Christmas Eve?"

She sighed. "Ridiculous, right?"

"More like suicidal." He looked at his watch. "I predict you'll be out of there in about four hours."

Four hours? Okay, so I'd been in denial that our plans for a quiet wedding had already been trampled underfoot by that steamroller some people call fate. But this information brought the unhappy truth crashing down on me like a Steinway falling from the top of the Transamerica Tower. And to add insult to devastating injury, I'd now be spending four hours in a mall—on Christmas Eve. I knew myself. I'd never last four hours in a mall. The last time I had to go shopping in one I nearly bought an Uzi at Toys R Us and went on a rampage to bust myself out.

"Come on." Clarissa yanked the sleeve of my jacket. "Let's get this show on the road."

The five of us linked hands and made our serpentine way into the mall. The interior was ablaze with light. Above the throngs of people I could see scores of giant, red candy canes and Styrofoam snow flakes the size of manhole covers. The cloying scent of cinnamon was overwhelming. Christmas music was blasting over hidden loudspeakers. At least, I think it was Christmas music. It was kind of hard to tell with all the ambient screaming going on.

I began to feel woozy.

"Clar?" I began.

She ignored me. "Over there." She pointed at something.

I looked around. "What?"

"Between Cinnabon and The Sunglass Hut," she clarified. "The men's restroom."

Alvin was insistently tugging at my hand. "I have to pee!"

I looked at Clarissa. "The *men's* restroom?"

"You can pull it off." She tossed her mane of red hair. "Channel your inner Rachel Maddow. We'll wait for you by the Sunglass Hut." She looked down at Simon and Teddy. "Won't we guys?"

They began to protest.

She sweetened the deal. "I'll buy you some Ray-Bans."

Simon shoved Teddy out of the way. "Move it lard-ass."

They took off toward the kiosk.

I sighed and embraced my fate. After all, how bad could it be?

I was about to find out.

Alvin and I stood in a long line that stretched out along the corridor that led to the men's room. There were men and boys in every shape, size, each sporting varying levels of discomfort. Most of them were complaining about how long it was taking to inch forward. A large guy in front of me was dictating text messages into his cell phone. *Loudly.*

He was built like a linebacker and was wearing a Ravens hoodie that was about five sizes too small for his massive frame. He kept backing

154

up while bellowing into his phone, so I had to keep yanking Alvin out of harm's way.

"Tell that skanky bitch she'd better be gone when I get back to the office." Pause. "Period."

Maybe the guy didn't realize how loud he was, and that there were kids all around us. I cleared my throat.

He turned around to glower at me.

"You got a problem?"

I shook my head. "No. But there *are* kids everyplace."

"Who gives a shit?" He turned back around and resumed his colorful dictation. "Carla is a cunt." Pause. "Exclamation point." He grunted and held his phone closer to his mouth. "Not fucking *can't*," he corrected. "*Cunt*. C-U-N-T."

Alvin looked up at me.

"What's a cunt, Diz?"

I was not having this conversation. Particularly not when a wall of surliness loomed just in front of us. I bent down to whisper to him. "We'll talk about it later, okay?"

Apparently, some guy in line behind us had another idea. "Why don't you watch your mouth, asshole?"

I straightened up just in time for Dick Butkus to wheel back around.

"Did you just call me an asshole?" he demanded. He stepped closer. His breath smelled like stale beer.

I stared up at him. "No. I don't believe I called you anything," I paused. "Ellipsis."

He narrowed his already beady eyes. "Are you being a smartass?"

Before I could compliment him on his powers of discernment, Alvin stepped into the void.

"Hey mister," Alvin tugged on the purple sleeve of his hoodie. "What's a cunt?"

Butkus glared down at him, then back at me. "You let your kid talk like that?" He jerked a fat thumb toward Alvin.

"No," I replied. "And he's not my kid."

Butkus wasn't buying it. "I recognize you, now." He continued to look me up and down. It made me feel itchy inside my clothes. "You're that bossy dyke from TV." He elbowed the guy standing beside him. "It's that liberal news bitch. What's her name?"

"Rachel Maddow," an alto voice behind me supplied.

I felt a tingle run up my spine—and it wasn't the good kind.

Clarissa.

I turned around to face her.

She was giving me that measured look of hers—the one that said, "What the hell have you done now?" I noticed that she had Simon and Teddy in tow—both wearing snappy new shades. Simon had Aviators. Teddy was sporting Wayfarers. They looked too cool for this corridor.

Alvin shifted his gaze to Clarissa. "What's a cunt?"

I raised a hand to my forehead. This was going to end badly.

Clarissa was chewing the inside of her cheek.

Butkus wasn't backing down, either. But I did notice he was having a hard time keeping his eyes off Clarissa.

She decided to defuse the situation by giving him her best, full-frontal Rita Hayworth.

"I'd like to apologize for the rudeness of my friend here. She isn't used to dealing with little boys in distress." She indicated Alvin, who now was holding onto his crotch with both hands. Clarissa gave Butkus a brilliant, just-between-us smile. "I'm sure *you* understand."

Butkus backed up and spread out his beefy arms. "Make way, everybody. This little lady has an emergency."

Clarissa beamed at him and took hold of Alvin's hand.

"Thank you, most kindly."

They pushed their way forward to the head of the line.

Butkus and I watched them go.

"Now that's a nice piece of ass," he said.

Although I wanted to punch his lights out, I was hard-pressed to disagree.

I dropped my gaze to Simon and Teddy, who looked like pygmy members of McGarrett's Five-O Task Force.

"Did you guys pick out some sunglasses for Alvin?"

Teddy nodded and held up a bag.

"Lemme see."

I took the bag and pulled out a pair of blinding white frames that contained lenses the size of dinner plates. "Coco Chanel?" I asked. "Seriously?"

Teddy shrugged.

Simon waved a hand. "He's a pervert. They'll go great with those Jimmy Choo's."

I couldn't really argue with him.

* * *

The line to Santa's Crystal Snow Palace snaked around the mall in an endless series of loops and doglegs. It was about a zillion degrees in that joint—and it was more crowded than a Mumbai commuter train.

I was hungry and my stomach kept growling.

"This is the fourth time we've passed that same Chick-fil-A," I complained.

"Deal with it. We're *not* giving up our place in line."

I sighed and decided to try another approach. *Bribery.*

I leaned closer to Clarissa. "How about we blow this pop stand and just take the kids to…" I looked around for the nearest store that would be likely to have an outside entrance. "*Cabela's.* We can buy them anything they want."

"Good idea." Clarissa raised a red eyebrow. "I'm sure the boys are running low on ammo."

I blew out an exasperated breath. "Come on, Clar. We're going to be stuck in this line for the rest of our natural lives."

"Diz." She glared at me unapologetically. "You're whining more than *any* of the kids in this line. Suck it up and deal with it."

It was true. I stubbed the toe of my shoe into the base of an obnoxious and overdone Styrofoam snowman that was staring down at me with a maniacal smile. It toppled over like a stack of Jenga blocks and took out an entire stand of cardboard spruce trees on its way down. Fake snow flew everywhere.

A kid behind us started screaming. "That man hurt Frosty!"

Oh shit.

Clarissa fixed me with a murderous gaze. "What did you do now?"

"She eighty-sixed the snowman," Simon explained.

"Hey? Shrimp boat?" I bent toward Simon and made rapid slashing motions beneath my chin. "Not helping."

The kid behind us was still screaming. Soon other tired, hungry and impatient kids joined in. It spread through the line like a wave. A chorus of yuletide rage drowned out the ambient *Best of Manheim Steamroller* tunes that had been playing for the last three hours.

I tried to placate the ringleader. She was still screaming and she had lungs like Ethel Merman on opening night.

"It's okay," I explained. "Frosty isn't hurt. He's just—lying down. He's *tired*. Like we all are."

Ethel wasn't buying it. Neither was her mother.

"What's the matter with you?" She hissed at me and picked up her yodeling spawn. "If you hate Christmas so much, then you shouldn't be here spoiling it for everyone else."

Hate Christmas? *Me?*

"Hey. Wait a second, lady," I began.

Clarissa took hold of my arm. "Diz?"

I shook her off. I'd had just about enough of this.

"Look lady, I didn't *ask* to be stuck in this sweltering line with five-hundred howling, midget refugees from hell."

"Daaaaaaddddyyyyyy!" her kid was screaming. "A mean man is attacking mama!"

What? I wasn't attacking anybody—certainly not this snotty-nosed kid who was wailing like a Banshee.

"Hold on a minute." I reached out to try and placate the squalling youngster. Her mother yanked her away from me like I was one of the Lindbergh kidnappers.

"You keep your hands off my child!" She was screaming now, too. "Help! Security! This man is trying to steal my baby!"

"What? No. *No!* That isn't what I'm—" It was pointless. "Hold on a minute…."

It was too late. I could see it all unraveling. *Of course.* It was like a bad reenactment of the worst moments of my life.

I heard the voice of my inner Elizabeth Bennet. *Were the same fair prospect to arise at present as had flattered them a year ago, every thing, she was persuaded, would be hastening to the same vexatious conclusion.*

158

I was toast, and I knew it. Maybe, with luck, I wouldn't end up in jail this time.

I looked at Clarissa with trepidation.

Okay. Maybe some time in jail wouldn't be such a bad thing.

Over Clarissa's red head, I could see bigger trouble headed my way. Bigger in the form of an angry linebacker, making a beeline for where we stood.

It was Butkus, all right. And he was mad as hell.

"Daaaaaaddddyyyyyy!" Little Ethel was still screaming and now flailing her sinewy arms toward my advancing fate.

"You!" he bellowed. "What the hell are you doing to my family, you pervert?"

"I'm not," I began to explain. *Waitadamnminute. Pervert?* "Hold on a minute, mister."

Butkus shoved me and sent me reeling as easily as if I had been another Styrofoam creation. I lost my footing and went sprawling into a field of Day-Glo candy canes.

Alvin, Simon and Theodore all gaped at me from behind their high-dollar shades.

"You didn't stick the landing," Simon said.

Clarissa scrambled over the makeshift fence and knelt beside me.

"Are you okay?"

I spat out a mouthful of fake snow.

"Do I look okay?"

"Come on," she started to help me up. "Let's get back in line."

Back in line? Was she suicidal or just crazy?

"Are you suicidal or just crazy?" I asked.

"Neither. Come on." She took hold of my forearms. "Stand up."

"Yeah," Butkus repeated. "Stand up and face me like a *man*."

Clarissa had had just about enough of this manufactured drama. She pursed her lips and confronted Butkus. No more Rita Hayworth. This time, he was getting her best Barbara Stanwyck.

"She's *not* a man. And it's worth noting that you aren't comporting yourself like much of one, either."

It took Butkus a while to work his way through that one to reach the implied insult. But he managed.

159

"Fucking dykes. You're fucking *everyplace*. You're what's wrong with this country."

I saw Clarissa square her shoulders.

Uh oh. "Clar...no!"

I scrambled to my feet to try and stop her, but I was too late.

"You insufferable, cretinous lout. The only affronts to 'traditional' family values present here tonight are your unbridled expressions of ignorance, bigotry and bad fashion sense." Clarissa took a step closer to him. "You and your unsavory ilk are the real crimes against nature."

I took hold of her shoulders. They felt like rods of rebar. "Honey," I began.

"Fucking queers. Fucking perverts." Butkus pointed at the boys. "Why does the fucking government let you people adopt kids and drag them out in front of *real* families at Christmas?"

"Actually," Simon lowered his Ray Bans and chimed in. "We're not adopted—and we're here under duress."

I rolled my eyes.

"Shut up, Simon."

Mrs. Butkus tsked. "You shouldn't be allowed to talk to children like that."

"I couldn't agree more," Clarissa faced her. "Why don't you and Cro Magnon man take your precious spawn and retreat to some other bastion of rarified air?"

Mrs. Butkus just blinked back at her. But Mr. Butkus was swelling with rage.

"Don't think I won't flatten your bitch wiseass just because you're a woman."

"I'd like to see you *try*," Clarissa thrust out her chin. "You loud-mouthed blowhard."

Shit. Dozens of people were now circling us—like turkey buzzards eyeing a fresh kill.

A couple of overweight mall security guards were making their way over from Chick-fil-A. I noticed that they were still carrying their super-sized drink cups.

"Clarissa?"

I could see Butkus sneer and draw back his arm—just like he was

160

getting ready to heave a Hail Mary pass down the field. With all my might, I shoved Clarissa out of the way just as he let it fly.

It was a textbook right cross, and it nailed me square on the jaw. I collapsed like a house of cards.

Strangely, before everything went blank, I thought I heard Ethel Merman singing "Baby, It's Cold Outside."

✿ ✿ ✿

"Sweetheart? Can you hear me? Come on, baby. Wake up."

I came to, slowly. Everything around me was still pretty hazy. The only thing I was sure about was that my head was being cradled in a nest of warm cashmere, and the air around me smelled like red violets.

"What happened?" I croaked.

"She's coming to," a man's voice said. "Hey, Demonte? She's waking up."

There were bright lights over me. I blinked my eyes to try and adjust them.

"Where are we?" I asked.

Clarissa stroked my hair. "In the mall. Remember?"

My face felt like it was on fire. I could barely move my jaw. I raised my hand to touch it and recoiled from the pain.

"Ow. That really hurts."

"I know." Clarissa took hold of my hand. "You're lucky it's not broken."

"Can she sit up?" It was the man's voice again.

"Can you try to sit up, sweetheart?"

Clarissa helped me roll up into a semi-erect position. The room was spinning less, and I could begin to make out the contours of gaudy Christmas decorations. Everything came flooding back in a rush.

"Shit. He slugged me, didn't he?"

Clarissa nodded. "You're going to have one hell of a bruise."

I looked around. "Where is he?"

One of the security guards jerked a thumb toward a nondescript exit. "Back there. Cooling off in our office."

"Where are the Blues Brothers?" I asked Clarissa.

161

"With Santa. He took pity on us when he found out about the fracas. He let them jump to the head of the line. They're up there having chicken nuggets and hot chocolate with his elves."

"Sheesh." I cradled my head in both hands. "I feel like death takes a holiday."

The larger of the two security guards cleared his throat. "We need to know if you intend to press charges."

"Yeah," the other one added. "Demonte and I hope you don't, ma'am. Negative publicity like that would be bad for the mall—and we'd probably lose our Christmas bonuses."

"Publicity?" I looked at Clarissa with confusion.

"They think you'll put it on your show." She smiled at me. "But I assured them that you wouldn't do that. Right, Rachel?"

Oh. Yeah. *Right.* "No. I wouldn't do that."

Demonte and his colleague let out grateful breaths.

"That's great, ma'am. Just great."

"We really like your show, too." Demonte asked. "Can we get you anything?"

I was about to ask for a couple of number one combos from Chick-fil-A, but for once, Clarissa beat me to the punch.

"I have a phone number for our Uber." She handed him a slip of paper. "Would you mind giving him a call and asking him to pick us up at the nearest entrance?"

"Sure." Demonte took the paper from her. He faced the other guard. "You wanna go get the kids for them?"

"Yeah," he said. "We'll meet you all at the exit back there," he pointed behind them. "Near Cinnabon."

"Come on, Rach." Clarissa helped me stand up. "I think our work here is through. Let's shake the dust from our feet and go home."

❄ ❄ ❄

It was close to eleven o'clock when we finally got home. Alvin and Teddy both fell asleep in their car seats—still wearing their sunglasses. Simon was alert as ever. The blue glow from his electronic Sudoku game illuminated the interior of the van. I rode most of the way home with my head pressed agains the cold window and watched the snow continue to fall. It was really piling up. Fortunately, most of the traffic had abated. There were only a few sets of tire tracks on the streets once we reached our neighborhood.

Clarissa parked in front of our house and shut off the engine.

Christa's house was dark. I hope that meant she had the evil canine twins tucked snugly into bed with her. It was about time something went my way.

It was quiet when we climbed out of the van. Peaceful. The night sky looked pink. It was so still I thought I could hear the snow falling.

Then from somewhere on the night air, a plaintive sound swirled around us. The hypnotic noise grew louder as we approached the house.

Clarissa was carrying Alvin. She halted and tipped her head toward the sound.

"Is that what I think it is?"

I shifted Teddy higher in my arms and stopped to listen, too.

Oh, god.

"It's Sadie," Simon explained. "It means she has to pee."

Clarissa and I exchanged glances.

I took the front steps two at a time and unlocked the door. Sadie came exploding out of the house like she'd been fired from a cannon. She dropped her back end to the ground and scooted around in crazed circles, leaving a dazzling sequence of bright yellow snow loops in her wake. When she finally finished and calmly trotted back up the steps, the front yard looked like it had been vandalized by a psychotic Spirograph.

I sighed. "I guess they're home."

There was a note taped to the front door. Clarissa pulled it off and opened it.

"Karl arrived early. They left for North Carolina tonight so they could get ahead of the winter storm."

"Winter storm?" I repeated. "What winter storm?"

"The one that's rolling up the coast from Georgia," Simon clarified. "I've been watching it all night on Weather Underground. It's due to the strong El Niño this year."

Right. Check. *Of course.* How could it be otherwise?

Clarissa smiled at me. "Buck up, baby. Let's make the best of it, okay?"

"Okay." It wasn't like I had much of a choice. And right then, all I wanted was to pack my aching jaw in ice and sleep for about nine years.

Once we were inside, Clarissa suggested we carry the still sleeping Alvin and Teddy straight upstairs. She got no argument from me. Together we undressed the boys and got them into their jammies. They protested when we took their sunglasses, however, and we had to promise them that they could have them back in the morning. Once they were tucked in, I faced Simon.

"You, too, bucko."

Simon was having none of it. "I want to watch Colbert."

"I don't think so."

"You didn't do Teddy's ear drops," he pointed out.

"Nice try. Get into your jammies. Now."

"Fine," he grumbled. "Don't blame me when his ear slime eats through the mattress."

That caught Clarissa's interest. "Diz?"

"Yeah, yeah. I'll go get 'em." I grabbed Simon by the collar of his shirt. "Come on, Einstein. You've got a date with a toothbrush."

"I'll meet you downstairs." Clarissa waved and left the guestroom.

"I'll be right behind you," I called out. "Warm up the Remy."

"I wouldn't advise that." Simon was taking off his pants. "It's risky to drink alcohol when you might have a concussion."

I handed him his pajamas. "Where'd you learn that?"

"Sheila."

His mom—of course. He'd probably picked it up from all the times she clobbered Marty.

"You're just a font of information, you know that?"

He finished brushing his teeth and got into his pajamas.

"I'd like to get up at six."

"Oh, yeah?" I replied. "I'd like to sleep until Tuesday. Wanna flip for it?"

He rolled his eyes.

We walked back into the bedroom. I held up the covers so he could climb into the big bed beside to his brothers.

164

"Do you want to help me get this stuff into Teddy's ears?"

"Not really."

He folded his Ray Bans and laid them on the nightstand.

I sat down on the edge of the bed.

"Dude?" I began. "It hasn't been a great night for me. Your dad got sick at work and heaved his guts out all over the car. I took you and your brothers to see Santa Claus on the busiest night of the year, and I ended up getting my clock cleaned by a gorilla in a purple sweatshirt. There's a blizzard brewing outside and it's likely that the five of us are going to be stuck inside this house with two psychotic dogs until the spring thaw. So unless you want to end up with a starring role in a remake of *The Donner Party*, I suggest you stow the attitude and start acting a little more like a team player."

He thought it over.

"I'll hold his head and you put 'em in."

Finally.

Teddy didn't fight us. *Much.* Let's just say that even in a sleep state, he kicked like a donkey and narrowly missed turning his brother into a soprano.

Soon I had them all settled down, and walked across the room to turn out the light.

"Sweet dreams, guys."

All I got in response were three sets of soft snores.

I walked past our bedroom on my way downstairs and noticed that Sadie and Maris were on our bed, snuggled together on our pillows.

Great.

I was halfway to the stairs before it registered with me that Maris had been wearing a sleep mask. I didn't even want to think about how that happened.

When I reached the living room, I noticed that the front door was standing open. And there was a huge tower of boxes piled up behind the sofa.

Clarissa came back inside and kicked the door closed behind her. Her hair was salted with snow and her arms were loaded with more boxes and a big, bulging bag of wrapping paper.

"What the hell is all of this?"

165

"What does it look like?" She set the boxes down on a table. "They're presents. For the kids."

Presents?

Oh, shit. *Their presents.* From Santa. Marty told me we'd have to wrap them all.

"What the hell did he do? Buy out Walmart?"

"I have no idea. But if we want to get all of this done before morning, we'd better get started."

I sagged onto a chair arm. "I don't have it in me, honey. Can't we just go to bed?"

I didn't bother to remind her that it was obvious we wouldn't be getting married tonight—or any night in the near future.

Clarissa walked over to where I slouched in misery and knelt before me.

"I know this isn't what we planned." Her voice was soft and low. "But, sweetheart? As trying as this all is, it's Christmas. They're kids and they don't have any choice in the matter. They can't be with their parents, so it's up to us to make the experience as special for them as possible." She laid a soft hand on the side of my face—the side that wasn't swollen to twice its normal size. "You and I will have the rest of our lives together. This is just one night."

I folded like a cheap suit.

"One night?"

She nodded.

"You promise?"

She nodded again.

I smiled. I was starting to feel a little like a kid myself. I bent toward her.

"You really wanna be with me forever?"

She rolled her eyes. "Most of the time."

I kissed her. It was wonderful. Just like kissing her always was.

We got a little more intent on the exercise. It was all going great except for the part that felt like someone was jabbing my face with a hot poker. Then it happened.

Tears stung my eyes. I pulled back reluctantly.

Clarissa thought I was crying. "Oh, honey. It's okay."

"No," I explained. "I'm not upthet. My faith hurth."

She raised an eyebrow. "Your what hurts?"

"My faith." I pointed at it.

"Diz?"

"Oh, thit."

Clarissa giggled.

"Thop it."

"What happened?"

I raised a hand to my face. "I bith my tongue."

Clarissa gave up trying not to laugh. She threw back her red head and just about bayed herself right out of her sweater. Even though I tried hard to be annoyed, I couldn't quite pull it off—not when so much unbridled magnificence was on display before me.

I gave her a sheepish smile and reached out to pull her closer.

"Wanna meth around?"

"Yes," she said. She was still chuckling. "Absolutely. *You bet*. Right after we wrap all those presents."

My shoulders sagged.

"Come on." She gave me a playful nudge. "I'll make us something to drink and you can turn on the Christmas tree and play that horrible music you love so much."

Horrible music? My face lit up.

"Really?"

"Yes, really. Vinnie Zimmerman, or whatever his name is. That abominable lounge lizard music."

"Thummo," I said.

"Pardon me?"

I sighed. "Hith name. Ith Thummo, not Thimmerman."

She patted my knee. "Of course it is, sweetheart."

She stood up and headed for the kitchen.

I sighed and decided I was better off simply to embrace my fate.

I plugged in the tree lights and got Vinnie spooled up. As soon as those retro Bossa Nova tones of "God Rest Ye Merry Gentlemen" started filling the room, I felt a lot better. The cool blue lights on the Christmas tree helped, too. They caused the dozens of tiny raven and cardinal ornaments to glow like they were internally illuminated.

It *was* Christmas, after all. And even though my face felt like it had gone ten rounds with an anvil, I was still here—in my own home. On Christmas Eve. With the love of my life.

I thought about Clarissa and the winding road we'd traveled to reach this place—this very place that was filled with so much peace and joy.

Hell. She was the love a thousand lifetimes.

I walked over to the towers of boxes and began to sort them by size. We'd just have to guess which gifts were for what kids. Simon's were pretty easy to pick out. Anything that had a line of type designating that the product was for "adults and children over age eighteen" was plainly for him. I decided that Alvin would get everything that posed a choking hazard—even though I was tempted to cart them all upstairs and present them all to Sadie. The rest would go to Teddy by process of elimination.

It seemed to be working out all right. When I finished, I had three piles that were pretty equal in size.

Clarissa came back from the kitchen carrying a tray loaded with two large drinks and some nosh. I noted that her food choices were somewhat eclectic. I pointed at a bowl of something bland-looking and…runny.

"What ith that?"

"Cream of wheat."

"Cream of…" I gave up trying to say it. "Why?"

She handed me a spoon. "Because I didn't think you'd be able to manage Bavarian pretzels or crudités."

Good thinking. As always.

I took the spoon from her and picked up the bowl. She'd even dusted the hot muck with brown sugar. I looked at her with cow eyes.

"I luff 'ou."

"Eat," she commanded. "You're going to need your strength."

"Id won be thath bad. I got 'em all sordeth ow." I pointed at the three piles. "Thee?"

She nodded and fixed me with one of her best, smoldering Hollywood looks.

Lauren Bacall this time.

"I wasn't talking about *now*. I was talking about later—*after* we finish wrapping the presents."

It suddenly felt like the floor had dropped out from beneath my feet.

"So," Clarissa had moved on. Katharine Hepburn was back in charge. She hauled Marty's giant plastic bag full of wrapping paper over and pulled out three rolls. "Do you want to start with hermaphrodite reindeer, crack-addict Santas, or serial-killer elves?"

"I'll thart with Alvinth." I said. "Thith one." I grabbed the roll that was festooned with fat, cartoon reindeer.

An hour later, we had them all finished and were just starting to arrange them beneath the Christmas tree when I head the sound of something that sounded like advancing thunder. It was coming from upstairs.

Uh oh.

Before I could react, Sadie came bounding down the stairs at warp six. She slid to a halt in front of the door seconds before we heard the telltale sound of feet stomping on the porch floor to knock snow from shoe tops. The doorbell rang.

Sadie began that earsplitting yodel of hers—that annoying, uniquely Siberian husky sound that was her breed's psychotic substitute for barking.

"What the hell?" Clarissa climbed to her feet. "*Sadie.* You hush. *Now.*" She hurried over to the door. "Who is it?"

"Baltimore police," a deep voice boomed. "Open the door, please, ma'am."

Clarissa looked at me with amazement. I shrugged.

She opened the door wide enough to peer around the chain lock. "May I see your IDs, please?"

They must've been legit, because Clarissa quickly closed the door and unlatched the lock.

She took hold of Sadie's collar and pulled the door all they way open. Two of the largest men I'd ever seen filled up the opening. They did not look happy about being out in a blizzard on Christmas Eve. In fact, they didn't look like they'd be happy any other time, either.

The larger of the two men was holding a folded sheet of paper.

"Are you Maryann Gillespie?" he asked.

"Maryann?" Clarissa sounded confused. "No."

"Thath me." I raised my hand like I was reporting for roll call in homeroom.

"You're Maryann Gillespie?" he demanded.

I nodded.

He stepped forward and thrust the paper at me.

"I have a warrant for your arrest."

"A what?" Clarissa was incredulous.

"An arrest warrant," he explained.

I opened the paper in stunned silence and scanned its contents.

"Youth gotta be kiddin' me."

"What?" Clarissa snatched the paper out of my hands. She looked it over. "A man named Benny Brenowitz is charging you with assault and battery?" She glared at me. "Who the hell is Benny Brenowitz?"

"Butkuth."

"Butkuth?" she repeated. Then her eyes widened with recognition. "You mean that loudmouthed lummox who slugged you at the mall?"

I nodded.

She faced the policemen. "That's *absurd*. He's the one who attacked her."

"We're not personally involved, ma'am. We're just here to take Miss Gillespie downtown."

"Downtown? You mean to jail? Tonight? As in right now?"

"Yes, ma'am. Right now." He looked at his watch. "If we hurry, you can maybe get up in front of the judge before night court shuts down for the holiday. Otherwise?" He shook his head. "It'll be Monday morning."

Monday morning? That would mean spending four nights in the slammer. On Christmas. Impossible.

On the other hand, it would be a new personal best for me.

"Lemme geth my coat."

Clarissa grabbed my arm. "Hold on a minute." She faced the policeman. "Look officer," she squinted at his nametag, "Officer Colodny. You can't seriously be thinking about locking her up because of some ridiculous set of trumped-up charges?"

He stared back at her without speaking. The seconds ticked by.

"Clar?"

She whipped around to face me.

"Ith better if I juth go with 'em."

"Maryann Gillespie, if you try to walk out of this house on Christmas Eve without *me*, you're going to be sporting a shiner on top of a cracked jaw."

I blinked. It was rare for Clarissa to make such public displays of attachment.

"Ith okay, honey," I began. But Clarissa cut me off.

"You are *not* leaving me here alone with those hooligans."

I looked down at Sadie who, for once, was standing there pretty calmly. It made sense. I mean, after all, it wasn't my first rodeo. She'd seen me get arrested before.

"They're noth thath bath, Clar." I pointed down at Sadie. "Thee?"

Clarissa rolled her eyes. "I wasn't talking about the *dogs*. I meant Marty's kids."

"Ma'am?" It was clear that Officer Colodny was growing exasperated. "We need to go. Now."

"I goth a go, Clar."

Clarissa sighed. "Where are you taking her?"

Officer Colodny handed her a card. "Circuit Court building. Bosley Avenue, Towson."

I retrieved my coat and faced the officers. "Do you neeth tha cuff me?" I asked.

"I don't know." He actually smiled at me. "Are you planning to escape?"

"Nuh uh."

He took hold of my elbow. "I think you'll do just fine like this."

"Wait a minute." Clarissa grabbed his arm. "You are *not* taking her without me."

Officer Colodny looked down at Clarissa's hand. "Ma'am, you need to let go of my arm."

I saw Clarissa's lip twitch. She tightened her grip.

"Ma'am. I'm not kidding. You need to let go of my arm right now."

Clarissa lifted her chin. "Suppose I don't?"

171

"Clar…." I could see where this was headed.

But Officer Colodny wasn't buying it. "Ma'am, I know what you're doing and it isn't going to work."

"Really?" Clarissa raised an eyebrow and reached for a half empty glass of Remy Martin XO that sat on the console table behind the sofa. "Okay. How about this?" Before anyone could stop her, she upended the tumbler and poured the cognac on his head. The amber waves ran down his broad forehead at a rate of about seven dollars per ounce.

I closed my eyes.

Twenty minutes later, Clarissa, all three boys, and both dogs were crammed into the back seat of a police cruiser with me as we made our snowy way to Towson for the second time that night.

❀ ❀ ❀

The only good thing I can say about getting busted on Christmas Eve is that you don't have to cool your heels for very long. Everyone is pretty much invested in fast tracking the proceedings so they can get the hell outta Dodge before the night shift ends at one a.m. They even had Christmas carols playing in the booking area.

Because we had the kids—and the dogs—in tow, they let us wait in a kind of anteroom until our cases were called up for arraignment.

Cases. Jeez. I wondered, idly, if Clarissa and I would be permitted to have conjugal visits in Brockbridge?

The kids were still sleepy and had stretched out along some wooden benches. Amazingly, they all managed to grab their sunglasses on the way out of the house. It wasn't until we got herded into this small room and they took off their coats to use as pillows that I noticed what Alvin was wearing.

I nudged Clarissa. "Is that one of your…you know?"

At least my tongue was working again.

"My what?" She took a closer look at Alvin. "Oh, my *god*. Where did he get that?"

"He sleepwalks," Simon volunteered. "You're lucky it wasn't the full peignoir set."

I raised a hand to my eyes.

This was a nightmare. One that just promised to go on and on.

"Go back to sleep, Simon." Clarissa handed him a twenty-dollar bill. "There's more where that came from."

He looked dubious.

"I have a trust fund," she clarified.

He took the money and rolled over onto his side, away from the light.

I shook my head.

"Will you relax?" Clarissa sounded amazingly calm, considering she'd just racked up her first arrest for assault. "I called Kirk and he's on his way down."

Kirk was the Wiley family attorney. In the last couple of years, I'd gotten to know him pretty well.

"What about Frank?" I asked her. She'd also called my brother, Father Frank, to come and retrieve the kids and the dogs and take them back to our house to wait on us.

"He said he'd be here as soon as the bingo game ended."

Bingo? He was letting us sit in the joint on Christmas Eve until his *bingo* game was over?

I started at her in disbelief. "Seriously?"

She shrugged. "He said if he canceled an event every time you got arrested, the diocese would shut down his parish."

"Sheesh. What about all those vows he took to help others in distress?"

"I don't think those included a requirement for bailing his sister out of the joint more than twice in the same decade."

"I don't see why not," I sulked.

"Look at the bright side." She took my arm and rested her red head on my shoulder. "We're together at Christmas. For once."

I had to smile at that. It was true. We *were* together. Here, in this stuffy, wood-paneled room that smelled vaguely like a bus station. And we even had three kids and two dogs. The whole thing did exude a sort of Norman Rockwell feeling.

All except for that part about aggravated assault and attacking a police officer.

I kissed the top of her head.

Red violets. The scent of her hair filled up my world. Just like it always did.

"I love you, you know."

"I know." She squeezed my hand. "I love you, too."

"I guess it's probably Christmas by now."

"I'd imagine so. It was nearly midnight when we got here." I yawned. "Do you want to try to sleep?"

Before she could answer, the door to our room creaked open.

"Gillespie and Wiley?" A stout woman with a battered clipboard waved her arm at us. "You're up."

We exchanged glances.

"Come on, move it." The matron was in no mood to indulge us. "You two are the last cases tonight."

Ten minutes later, the five of us were herded into a dimly lighted courtroom to greet our fate.

I blinked when I saw the man seated in the judge's chair behind the bench. He had a long white beard and was wearing a bright red suit.

I nudged Clarissa. "Do you see what I see?"

She gave me an ironic look.

Two men were waving at us from one of the long tables at the front of the room.

Kirk and Frank. *Thank god.*

We walked forward to meet them.

"Hi ya, Diz." Frank was wearing his collar. *Nice touch.* "I sure as heck hope you look better than the other guy."

"Hi, Frank. Thanks for coming." I shrugged. "Again."

He laughed and leaned forward to kiss Clarissa on the cheek. "I thought you knew better than to follow in her footsteps?"

She smiled at him. "I've traveled worse roads."

He nodded and punched me on the arm.

"Can you hang with the kids and the dogs until we get this sorted out?" I asked him.

"Sure." He took the leashes from me. "Your buddy Kirk doesn't think it'll take very long. We'll wait in the back row. And, Diz?"

I looked at him.

"You're *so* taking us all to Waffle House when we get outta here."

I handed him Maris's sleep mask.

"What the blazes is this?" He held it up.

"Don't ask."

He shrugged and stuffed it into his coat pocket. He waved at the judge. "Nice job tonight. See you around, Tony."

The judge waved back. "Later, Frankie."

Frank winked at me and herded the dogs and the boys toward a bench at the back of the courtroom.

Clarissa was already deep in conversation with Kirk. He was showing her some paperwork and shaking his head.

"I don't care what it costs," I heard her whisper. "We are *not* spending Christmas in the joint. *Fix it.* Even if you have to pay that bastard off."

Kirk turned pale. "*Clarissa.* Do not talk about a police officer that way." He lowered his head closer to hers. "Not *here.*"

"What police officer? I was talking about that numbskull Brenowitz."

"Hear ye, hear ye," the bailiff bellowed. "All persons having business before the circuit court of the county of Baltimore are admonished to draw near and give their attention, for the Court is now in session. The honorable Judge Anthony Krzyzewski is presiding."

Kirk touched Clarissa's elbow. "Here goes."

The bailiff approached the bench and handed the judge a couple of file folders.

"Gillespie and Wylie, please approach the bench."

We both looked at Kirk for direction and he urgently waved us forward.

We stood there in silence while the judge flipped through the pages in our folders. He cleared his throat once or twice.

I glanced nervously at Clarissa and was surprised to see her trying not to smile.

The judge looked down at us.

"Miss Wylie?" he said. "Lovely to see you again. I must say that I wish it were under better circumstances."

"As do I, Your Honor." Clarissa sounded almost contrite. "I never did get to properly thank you for taking such good care of the children during that fracas at the shopping mall."

He actually chuckled. "Don't worry about that. It made getting stuck with that graveyard shift worth the effort." He shifted his gaze to me. "How's your jaw," he smiled, "Miss *Maddow?* That Brenowitz really nailed you."

"Um." I looked back and forth between Clarissa and the oddly dressed judge. "Am I missing something here?"

"Judge Krzyzewski was the Santa Claus at the mall," she explained. "When you got socked by that—"

Kirk cleared his throat.

Clarissa took the hint. "Gentleman," she corrected.

"Oh." I looked at him. "Really?"

"Yes, really," he explained. "I'm going to take pity on you, Miss Gillespie, and dismiss these charges. Partly because it's Christmas, and partly because Benny Brenowitz is a bad-tempered, obnoxious ass who persistently clutters my docket with his inane personal injury claims. You, on the other hand," he shifted his fatherly gaze to Clarissa. "You assaulted a Baltimore city police officer. That offense I cannot overlook."

Clarissa dropped her eyes. "I understand, Your Honor."

"Is the arresting officer present in the courtroom?" he asked.

"Yes sir, I am," a voice boomed from the back of the room.

"Come forward, please, Officer Colodny."

The big policeman strode forward and stopped beside us in front of the bench.

"Is this the woman who," he consulted his paperwork, "dumped a glass of liquor on your head?"

Officer Colodny nodded. "Yes, Your Honor."

The judge regarded Clarissa. "What do you have to say for yourself, young lady?"

Clarissa faced the policeman. "I am sorry about that. Truly." She looked up at the judge. "I have no excuse. No way to defend my actions. This entire night was never supposed to unfold the way it did." She reached out and took hold of my hand. "We were supposed to be enjoying a quiet Christmas Eve—just the two of us. Alone. For once." She lowered her voice. "We were going to get married tonight.

We hadn't told anyone but Father Frank, Diz's brother. He was going to be our only witness. But Marty got sick and Diz had to take his kids. So we put our plans on hold. The boys hadn't seen Santa yet, so we brought them to the mall, where we met you, and...well. You know the rest."

Judge Krzyzewski stared at her in silence for a moment. Then he cleared his throat.

"What led you to assault this officer?"

"I just didn't want to be away from Diz. Not tonight. And I knew there'd be no other way we'd all get to come along with her."

"Yes." He looked toward the back of his courtroom. "I noticed that you brought the entire menagerie." He nodded. "I have a Siberian husky myself. Wonderful dogs."

I opened my mouth to say something, but Clarissa stomped on my foot.

"Officer Colodny?" The judge faced the policeman. "What would it require for you to accept this beleaguered woman's sincere apology and withdraw your complaint?"

The policeman hesitated.

"And while you deliberate, may I remind you, Officer, that it is now," the judge consulted his watch, "twenty minutes to one on Christmas morning."

Officer Colodny sighed and turned to face Clarissa.

"That was some pretty tasty brandy," he said.

Clarissa beamed at him. "You liked it?"

He nodded. "I wouldn't say 'no' to a bottle to give the missus."

"I think I can take care of that," she said. "If we can find a liquor store that's still open and hasn't been robbed, I'll buy you two."

"Trust me, lady," the policeman said. "One thing I know how to find is an open liquor store."

"So. Are we quits?" the judge asked. "Everybody satisfied?"

Clarissa and Officer Colodny both nodded.

"Great." The judge banged his gavel. "Cases dismissed. This court is now out of session. Merry Christmas to all, and to all a good night."

I stared up at him in amazement. "That's it? We get to go home?"

He got to his feet and put on his red Santa hat. "Not quite. There's one more small matter of business we need to attend to before the two of you can leave."

He came down from the bench and walked over to stand in front of us.

"Hey, Frank?" he called out to my brother. "You want to bring those children up here?"

He smiled at me. "We need a few witnesses for this wedding."

Wedding? I looked at Clarissa. She tightened her grip on my hand. Frank and the boys had joined us.

"Alrighty, then." Judge Krzyzewski cleared his throat. "Who gives this woman to be wed?"

As if on cue, Sadie cut loose with one of her textbook, ear splitting chirps. Clarissa and I exchanged startled glances.

The judge laughed.

"Works for me," he said.

✿ ✿ ✿

By the time we got home, there were only few hours remaining until dawn. The snow was still falling, but more slowly—in fat, fluffy flakes. The world around us looked—*different*. It was reborn. Like a village made of marzipan. Everyday things seemed richer, sweeter, full of innocence and alive with promise.

We did manage to find an all-night liquor store that hadn't been robbed, and Clarissa gifted Officer Colodny with two big, shiny bottles of Remy Martin XO. He joined us for an early wedding breakfast at Waffle House—along with Frank and the kids. We bought a cheeseburger for Sadie, and a black bean burger for Maris, who was reputed to be vegan—her fondness for pork tenderloin, notwithstanding. The dogs were content to doze on the backseat of the cruiser, contentedly listening to police band radio.

Luckily for us, it was a busy night in Baltimore.

Once we got back to the house, we were all so exhausted that we decided not to fight the boys about pajamas, retainers, or eardrops. We just collapsed into our bed in one big, giant, happy heap with promises that when we woke up, we'd open presents, trudge through the snow to visit Marty, and eat junk food all day.

Falling asleep in those last hours of night with Clarissa's head on my shoulder, and surrounded by the soft snores of three kids and two dogs, I thanked the lone, lucky star that had managed to guide me to this quiet place of peace and great joy. Somehow, without my knowledge, the bleakness of my lonely nevermore had morphed into evermore. Something simpler, wiser—filled with soft blue light and the sweet, enduring scent of red violets.

It was enough.

Backcast

"*Backcast* is a memorable story about the unbreakable strength and resilience of women. Skillfully executed, the story is easy to become emotionally invested in, with characters that are guaranteed to entertain and enthrall."   —*Lambda Literary Review*

"I love Ann McMan."
                —Dorothy Allison, author of *Bastard Out of Carolina*

Backcast by Ann McMan
Print 978-1-61294-063-2
Ebook 978-1-61294-064-9

www.bywaterbooks.com

About the Author

ANN McMAN is the author of seven novels, *Jericho, Dust, Aftermath, Hoosier Daddy, Festival Nurse, Backcast* and the forthcoming *Goldenrod*, and the short story collections *Sidecar* and *Three*. She is a recipient of the Alice B. Lavender Certificate for Outstanding Debut Novel and a four-time winner of Golden Crown Literary Society Awards. Her novel, *Hoosier Daddy*, was a Lambda Literary Award finalist. She resides in Winston-Salem, North Carolina with her wife, two dogs, two cats, and an exhaustive supply of vacuum cleaner bags.

Bywater
BOOKS

At Bywater Books we love good books about lesbians just like you do, and we're committed to bringing the best of contemporary lesbian writing to our avid readers. Our editorial team is dedicated to finding and developing outstanding writers who create books you won't want to put down.

We sponsor the Bywater Prize for Fiction to help with this quest. Each prize winner receives $1,000 and publication of their novel. We have already discovered amazing writers like Jill Malone, Sally Bellerose, and Hilary Sloin through the Bywater Prize. Which exciting new writer will we find next?

For more information about Bywater Books and the annual Bywater Prize for Fiction, please visit our website.

www.bywaterbooks.com

CPSIA information can be obtained
at www.ICGtesting.com
Printed in the USA
LVOW12s0612291216
518954LV00004B/18/P